"I can't afford to spend my whole life on the run, Joe, so if you don't have a plan, it looks like I'll have to make one."

"Okay," he answered, folding his arms as he waited. And waited. "You don't have one either, do you?"

Kate put her hands over her face and shuddered. "I don't want to give up my life, the children's life. I want to be able to go home. Plans are for starting over. I don't want to start over," she wailed.

Joe didn't hesitate. He pulled her over and put his arms around her. "We'll think of something, Kate."

She laid her head against his chest, enjoying the feel of his physical strength, the soapy smell of his recent shower, the man fragrance that she recalled from waking in his bed. She wanted to trust him. Had to trust him. There was no one else.

Dear Harlequin Intrigue Reader,

You wanted MORE MEN OF MYSTERY by Gayle Wilson—now you've got 'em! Gayle's stories about these sexy undercover agents have become one of Harlequin Intrigue's most popular ongoing series. We are as impressed by her outstanding talent as you, her readers, and are thrilled to feature her special brand of drama again in *Her Private Bodyguard* (#561). Look for two MORE titles in August and November 2000.

Also available this month, *Protecting His Own* (#562) by Molly Rice, an emotional story about the sanctity of family and a man's basic need to claim what's his.

There's no more stronger bond than that of blood. And Chance Quarrels is determined to see no harm come to the little daughter he never knew he had as Patricia Rosemoor continues her SONS OF SILVER SPRINGS miniseries with *The Lone Wolf's Child* (#563).

Finally, veteran Harlequin Intrigue author Carly Bishop takes you to a cloistered Montana community with a woman and an undercover cop posing as husband and wife. The threat from a killer is real, but so is their simmering passion. Which one is more dangerous…? Find out in *No Bride But His* (#564), a LOVERS UNDER COVER story.

Pick up all four for variety, for excitement—because you're ready for a thrill!

Sincerely,

Denise O'Sullivan
Associate Senior Editor
Harlequin Intrigue

Protecting His Own
Molly Rice

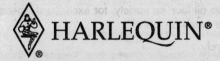

HARLEQUIN®

TORONTO • NEW YORK • LONDON
AMSTERDAM • PARIS • SYDNEY • HAMBURG
STOCKHOLM • ATHENS • TOKYO • MILAN • MADRID
PRAGUE • WARSAW • BUDAPEST • AUCKLAND

ISBN 0-373-22562-8

PROTECTING HIS OWN

Copyright © 2000 by Marilyn Schuck

Visit us at www.eHarlequin.com

Printed in U.S.A.

ABOUT THE AUTHOR

Molly Rice dreamed of becoming a chef...an architect...a scientist...an artist...a private detective...an actress...a psychologist....

Thanks to her writing, she can be anything she wants when she sits down to create lives for her characters. The research alone satisfies her tremendous thirst for knowledge and her insatiable curiosity about other people's lives.

In real life she has achieved a B.F.A. with a major in painting, written advertising copy, acted in a locally produced film, been a pastry chef and caterer, managed a paddle wheeler excursion company, been a bookkeeper, designed a complete kitchen and restored a 125-year-old Victorian minimansion, raised three children and published six books.

Is she satisfied? No! There are too many areas she hasn't explored, hasn't experienced. It may be too late for her to become a government secret agent, but in her next book...

Books by Molly Rice

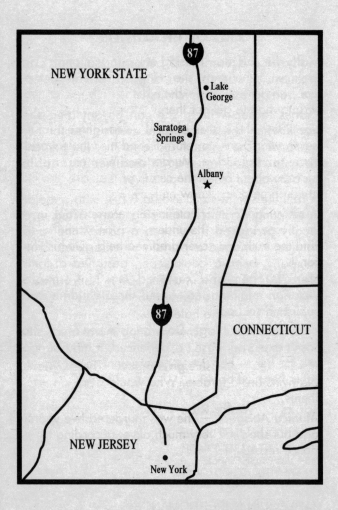

CAST OF CHARACTERS

Katelynn Adams — Raising another woman's children as her own, she will go to the ends of the earth to protect them — but what if she's trusted the wrong man to get her there?

Joe Riley — He's been abroad on assignment for seven years, only to return to find his whole world turned upside down. Murder and mayhem surround him, but at the center of it all are the children he didn't know he had....

Matt Wilkins — A private investigator, he took on Joe's case because he understood Joe's need to find the truth. He never dreamed he'd give his life for it.

Springer — He's a man with a foot in both camps. He's exchanged his freedom for his life and has plenty of reasons to hate the woman who is the cause of his bondage. Does he hate her enough to kill her?

Robbie Lee and Ashleigh Morgan — The six-year-old twins are adorable. Who would want to hurt them?

Monica Abrigado — She was murdered five years ago but she's still very much alive, according to police records.

Prologue

Kate tucked the blanket under Ashleigh's chin and ran a gentle finger down the child's plump, silken cheek. The nine-month-old baby gazed up at Kate with trusting blue eyes and hummed contentedly as she pursed her lips and pulled at the bottle nipple. Kate moved to the other crib and handed a bottle to Ashleigh's twin brother. Robbie grinned and snatched the bottle from her hands, gurgling something that sounded like ma-ma-ma.

"No, Kate—Kate—Kate," Kate said, brushing silken curls off his forehead. "Mama's at work."

But Robbie was already gurgling around the nipple. She smiled and pulled his blanket up.

She stood at the door, listening to the nursing sounds for a moment before turning off the light. A night-light glowed from the wall plug between the cribs. The babies turned on their sides, gazing at each other through the wooden bars as they drank their night bottles, their connection affirmed as it was every night at bedtime.

"Love you guys," Kate whispered, tiptoeing from the room. She loved these evening hours alone with the babies while Monica was at work, loved the feeling of responsibility. It seemed impossible that she'd an-

swered that ad for night baby-sitting in exchange for
rent only six months ago. Such a short time for Monica
and the twins to become her family.

She left the door slightly ajar and headed for her own
room. They were doing an extra hour of her favorite
TV show tonight; she'd catch the last half of it and
then, before she took her own shower, she'd mop up
the near flood that had resulted from the babies' exuberant baths.

The pile of envelopes on her nightstand reminded
her of the other part of her arrangement with Monica.
She switched on the TV and reached for the first envelope, the electric bill. She wrote out the check Monica had already signed and filled in the figure in the
stub. As she reached for an envelope she knocked the
checkbook off the nightstand. Something had slipped
from the pocket. As she started to push it back in she
saw that it was Monica's social security card. She
shook her head. Not the most secure place to keep the
card; it could be easily lost. She pushed it back in,
making a mental note to caution Monica. She reached
for the next bill.

After she had completed the task, with intermittent
pauses to enjoy her show, and had just popped the
sealed and stamped envelopes into her bag to be mailed
in the morning, the phone rang.

She snatched it up, laughing. "Yeah, Monica, I remembered and they're all d—"

"Katie! Listen to me!"

"I'm right here, Monica, you don't have to scream
in my ear," she scolded, holding the phone away.

The urgency in her roommate's voice rent the air.

"Kate, listen to me. You've got to get the kids and
get out of there!"

Kate pressed the phone back to her ear, swinging around to sit on the edge of the bed. "Get out…what do you…?"

"Kate, there's no time to talk…just do what I tell you. Shove a bunch of diapers and stuff in a bag, get the kids in your car and leave right away. There are some people…listen, you're in danger, we're all…if these guys get there before…"

Monica's voice trailed off and Kate began shouting her name. "Monica? What guys? Monica? Mon—"

"Yeah, yeah, I'm here…it's okay…I thought I heard…listen, Kate…there's a video case…it's the one labeled *Gone with the Wind*…take the money out of it, and Kate, there's a key taped to the bottom of the shelf in my closet…back corner against the wall…take it with you…Kate…are you listening?"

"I'm listening, but Monica, where am I supposed to—"

"Just go, Kate!" Monica's panic had already penetrated; Kate had been shoving her legs into her jeans as she clutched the phone to her ear with her shoulder and had already flung open her closet door to search for her backpack.

"How will you know where we've gone, Monica?"

"When you get somewhere…wait!" Another of those frightening pauses and then Monica came back on the line.

"Put an ad in the personals column of the *Daily*…I'll watch for it and contact you. Kate…go!"

Kate tore through the apartment, making sure she had everything she'd need for an overnight stay with the babies in tow. She spotted Monica's checkbook where she'd left it on the nightstand and grabbed it on her way out, shoving it into her bag as she ran.

The babies were fractious, Kate's fright palpable enough to reach them as she struggled to get them down the stairs, whispering soothing words in a shaky voice, their diaper bags thumping against her hips, her backpack riding high on her shoulders, her breathing harsh and loud in the dimly lit stairwell.

The Volvo started at the first twist of the key and then died when she attempted to back out of the space. She pounded the steering wheel and forced herself to calm down with deep breathing and muttered prayers. The twins were crying in unison now, and she shut out the sound, concentrating to hear the sound of the engine. It turned over and she backed out, keeping one eye on the street and one on the rearview mirror.

There was no traffic on the street, no lights in any windows but those she'd left on in their apartment in her haste to get away. Her foot trembled on the brake pedal as she halted for the stop sign.

The key! She'd forgotten to take the key. She glanced again in her rearview mirror. Did she dare chance going back for it?

But just then she heard the screech of tires at the other end of the block, saw a dark car pull up in front of her building, saw three men jump out and head for the stairs. She pressed her foot to the pedal and maneuvered the car at reckless speed down the car-lined streets, ignoring stop signs, praying she'd make it to the highway without hitting something or someone on the way.

She joined the slight flow of traffic onto the highway with an explosive sigh of relief and shouted her triumph. Her yell startled the babies into an abrupt silence.

"Okay, guys, we made it. We're on our way."

She kept watch in the rearview mirror, making sure she wasn't being followed. Traffic was intermittent at this hour, and she reminded herself she wouldn't know if she was being followed, anyway. She was headed north. Four years of making this trip to work made her sense of direction instinctive, though she'd lost her job at Hudson River Excursions just three weeks ago.

For a moment her mind flashed back to the strange events leading up to the shut down of the company for which she'd worked for all that time. All the crew and office personnel had gone over to the bar across the street for lunch, their usual Friday practice. When they'd returned, the building had been under siege by IRS agents who'd allowed them, under careful surveillance, to remove only personal belongings. For Kate, that had meant the picture that always sat on her desk—the last recorded moment in her parents' lives before they'd died in the car accident on their way home from her graduation. In the picture, she wore her cap and gown and her parents each had an arm around her, grinning with pride. Even tonight, it was the first thing she'd shoved into her backpack before stuffing in underwear, jeans and shirts. She felt their loss with new pain as she realized that now, tonight, when she most needed them, she couldn't run to them, no longer had a home to run to.

The coincidence struck her. In less than a month she'd been forced out of her job and now out of her house. But surely this was only temporary. She'd stop in an hour or so and call the apartment. Monica would answer and assure her it had all been a bizarre mistake, and then Kate could come on back. But recalling the sheer panic in Monica's voice, she knew she was clutching at straws as fear rose to clutch at her throat.

She glimpsed the steady stream of car lights behind her and switched lanes. Nobody else changed lanes. She took a second to glance over her shoulder. The babies had nodded off.

Worst-case scenario: Monica was in real trouble and somehow it had spilled over onto her roommate and children. She fought back the tears. No way was she going to further endanger the twins by trying to drive through tear-blurred vision. To keep her mind focused on the road and away from her frightening thoughts, she sang old-favorite songs to herself for hours, as she drove farther and farther north.

It was five in the morning when she spotted the motel with the vacancy sign blinking its reminder of her own exhaustion. The babies, lulled by the car's motion, had not awakened. They'd probably sleep right through the move from car to bed. She could maybe get two hours' rest before they'd waken, wanting breakfast.

SHE WAS ALMOST ASLEEP, the babies curled into each other between her and the chair she'd pushed against the bed to act as a side rail, when her mind insisted on a recap of the night's events to consider her situation. She'd started to dial their home phone number before she settled in, but something had warned her off before she could finish making the connection.

Could those men who'd stormed their building have been cops? Could Monica be in trouble with the law? But no, she'd specifically said they were all in danger. So that meant... Her breath caught on a quickly stifled gasp as she envisioned the worst.

It had to have something to do with Monica's job singing at the Kismet Club. Kate had never felt comfortable with her friend's associations there, but Monica had pooh-poohed her fears, assuring her that her boss, Don Springer, wasn't about to let any harm come to her. The implication was that Monica and Springer had a thing going, that she was under his protection. Kate had never liked that thought, either, but had kept her doubts to herself.

She turned on her side and stared at the light blinking through the gap in the drapes. Her purse was a dark lump on the table in front of the window.

Her eyelids drifted down, heavy with the grit of fatigue. Suddenly they popped open as she thought about the money she'd found in the video case. In her rush to find it and get out, she'd only vaguely registered the heft of it, had no idea how much was actually there. She slipped out of bed and went to her purse. She'd shoved the money to the bottom, and then had run to get the twins out of their cribs.

Counting it in the dim light provided by the neon vacancy sign outside her window, she was surprised to see that it amounted to a little over four thousand dollars. A lot of money to have lying around the apartment, even in such an ingenious hiding place. How had Monica managed to save so much? She was reminded of the blithe manner in which Monica had suggested she quit looking for another job and hire on as the twins' full-time nanny, at the same salary she'd been earning at Hudson River Excursions. At the time, Kate had protested that Monica couldn't afford that, and Monica had smiled that enigmatic smile and told her not to worry about it.

Kate put the money back in her purse and returned on tiptoe to the bed. She fell asleep worrying about the money, about where Monica had got it, about where she should go, how far from New York City she should travel, how long it would take Monica to contact her after Kate put the ad in the paper.

She awoke with a jolt as the television blared to life and the children yelled in response. Someone, a maid or the previous tenant, must have left the timer on, causing the TV to automatically come on at 7:00 a.m. Kate scrambled for the remote to lower the volume just as the TV anchor announced the discovery of a young woman's body in the alley behind the Kismet Club in Manhattan.

Pulling the babies into her arms, Kate rocked them back and forth as tears spilled down her cheeks. "My poor angels," she sobbed, as she pressed the off button on the remote, "what's going to become of you now?"

There was no doubt in her mind that Monica Abrigado was dead.

Ashleigh put her hand on Kate's wet cheek. "Mama-ma," she said. This time Kate didn't correct the baby.

SHE WAS NEVER ABLE to look back and recall the next hour in that motel room. But during the time she added hot tap water to boxed cereal in plastic drinking cups, opened jars of banana baby food, got their spoons out of a diaper bag and propped the babies in an armchair to feed them, she must have pulled herself together to accomplish all she did.

In fact, as she spooned food into the children, her mind went to work to analyze her position. First, she had no idea if Monica's death changed anything; she had to assume she and the children were still in danger. Second, she couldn't go to the police; the first thing they would do is turn the babies over to Child Protection. Neither she nor Monica had any living family, it had been one of the common bonds that formed a friendship out of what had started as an agreeable business arrangement. With Monica gone, the children had no one but Kate. They knew her and she loved them; the idea of having them sent to strangers, possibly separated from each other, horrified her.

She envisioned the stream of traffic at her back, bad guys, cops, maybe even the FBI if they considered her a kidnapper.

That was when the idea formed. If there were hunters behind her, her best bet was to stop in her tracks and let them go right on past her. They'd be expecting her to go as far as she could as fast as she could. And they'd be looking for her Volvo.

She had checked in for one night, paid cash in advance, incurred no extra charges. Checkout time wasn't until eleven. By eight thirty she'd gotten the kids back into their car seats, repacked and loaded the car, left the room key on the desk by the door and driven away from the small town.

In under thirty minutes she arrived in Albany and drove through neighborhoods until she found a house with a sign advertising licensed child care. She didn't like the idea of trusting the twins to strangers, but right now she had no choice. She left the children with a young woman who already had four small children in her care, promising that she'd be back for the twins in two hours. Next she drove around until she spotted a car parked on the street with a For Sale sign in the window. She parked the Volvo six blocks away and walked back. She called the phone number on the sign, then met with the owner. She paid seven hundred dollars in cash for the beat-up '82 Mercury and accepted the title, which she had no intention of filing. She drove

to where she'd parked the Volvo, transferred baby seats
and bags to the Merc, took the license plates off the
Volvo and drove away. She picked up the children at
exactly eleven and drove across town to a shabby old
building with a Furnished Apartment For Rent sign in
the window of the first-floor front apartment.

She stayed there for two weeks, hardly ever leaving
except to buy groceries at the small supermarket a
block away. She passed the time taking care of the
babies, studying the local and NYC newspapers and
reading the want ads. The apartment didn't come with
a TV, but she bought a cheap radio and kept it tuned
to a news station.

Once, when an announcer had given Monica Abrigado's name, Kate almost lost it even though she'd
known all along that her roommate had been murdered.
But she pulled herself together, brushed away the last
of her tears and listened carefully to the rest of the brief
news story. The police had found Monica's murderer.
Did that mean she and the children were safe? She had
no assurance of that and wasn't taking any chances.
But she felt it was time to go to phase two of her plan.

She had paid a full month's rent on the apartment;
the super wouldn't bat an eye when he discovered
she'd moved out after only two weeks.

Chapter One

Joe Riley stood in front of the dry cleaning establishment and looked over at the brownstone across the street. The building didn't seem to have suffered the ravages of time; both it and the street seemed, if anything, more upscale than he remembered.

What were the chances that Monica still lived there? Slim to none, probably. But on the chance that she did, how would she react to an old friend—an old lover—showing up after seven years of no communication whatsoever?

What the hell, what did he have to lose? A little face if she slammed the door in it? He crossed over, dodging a yellow cab on his right, a city bus on his left.

He'd only been here a couple of times back then, but he recalled there was a tenant roster in the foyer.

A man came up out of the basement well just as Joe started up the cement steps. He was carrying a trash bag and a broom. The super, Joe figured. The man glowered at him, his face creased with suspicion.

Joe nodded toward the front door.

"Looking for an old friend," he said.

The super shrugged and moved toward the Dumpster at the side of the building.

No Monica Abrigado listed. Joe's shoulders slumped with disappointment though he'd known, when he'd found no phone listing for her, that she'd probably long since moved on. Probably married by now. She'd been having an on-and-off thing with her boss at that club where she worked. She'd probably gone back to him after Joe was transferred to Saudi Arabia to work as a petroleum geologist.

What the hell, he hadn't really expected he could pick up his old life after a seven-year absence from the States.

The super came around the corner as Joe reached the sidewalk.

"Everybody works," the man muttered, passing Joe.

"I don't think my friend lives here anymore, anyway," Joe said.

The man stopped and stared at Joe. "Ain't nobody moved in the last couple years," he said.

"Been longer than that," Joe said. "I've been out of the country for the past seven years."

The super laughed, exposing missing teeth. Those remaining were stained by nicotine. "Ain't kept up on your correspondence, eh?"

Joe's answering grin was sheepish. "Something like that." He turned away.

"Hey," the super called after him.

Joe turned back.

"Who was you lookin' for, anyways?"

"Monica Abrigado. She used to live up in 2A."

A puzzled look crossed the super's face. "Abrigado? You knew her?"

Joe nodded. "You remember her?"

"Pretty hard to forget under the circumstances." The

man pulled a cigarette from his shirt pocket and stuck it in the corner of his mouth. He fumbled for matches.

Joe took a step toward him. "What circumstances?"

"Murdered," the man said around the cigarette as he found the matches and struck one.

"Murdered? Are you sure we're talking about the same woman?" Joe, feeling his equilibrium slipping, reached out to grasp the iron rail.

"Yep." The other man exhaled gustily and shook his head. "About six years ago. Went to work and didn't come back. Found her body next morning. Roommate disappeared, too."

Joe shook his head. "She didn't have a roommate when I knew her."

"Had one when she got herself kilt," the super insisted. He took a couple of quick drags and squinted his eyes at Joe. "Cops thought when she disappeared she mighta had somethin' to do with the murder."

A sensation of vertigo washed over Joe. He felt as if he'd wandered into the twilight zone.

Still clutching the rail, Joe fell more than sat on the bottom step. He heaved a sigh of frustration in the other man's direction. "Can you start at the beginning?"

"Abrigado didn't come home from work. Middle of the night the roomie disappears, too. Next day, the cops find Abrigado's body, come around lookin' for the roomie. She's gone. Disappeared." He threw the butt to the sidewalk, ground it out beneath his heel and then bent and picked it up.

It took a moment for Joe to process what the man had told him. Monica dead. Killed by her roommate? Why?

"Did they ever find her?"

The super shook his head. "Dunno. Probably

stopped lookin' when they found the guy that done it, though.''

''They found the guy…who was it?''

Another shake of his head as the elderly man reached for another smoke. ''Some mob soldier as I recall. Somethin' to do with that place she worked, maybe.''

Joe stood up. If he wanted the whole story, without the frustration, there were better places to go for it.

''Where's the nearest precinct?'' he asked the super.

''Couple a blocks that way,'' he said, nodding to his right, ''up Fourteenth.''

Joe nodded. ''Thanks.''

''Sure.'' He started to turn away and then hesitated. ''Say, ya think after all this time it's okay if I unload that stuff in the basement?''

''What stuff?''

''The stuff those women left behind. Had to put it in a storage locker down there. Nobody's come to claim it and the cops didn't seem too interested, and it would bring in a few bucks.''

Joe scratched his head, his mind still spinning. ''I dunno. Why not, if nobody's claimed it?''

The super took up the broom from where he'd laid it against the rail. ''Good money for kids' stuff nowadays, and them cribs are like brand new.''

''I don't see why n…'' His words trailed away as his mind caught up with what the super had just said.

''Cribs…kids' stuff? What are you talking about?''

''Them twin babies Abrigado had… never even took the cribs with 'em when they disappeared.''

Joe grabbed the other man by the arm, his frustration soaring out of control. ''What are you talking about?'' he shouted, unmindful of the alarm on the smaller man's face.

Five minutes later Joe was tearing up the street in search of the police precinct. And ten minutes after that, he was being directed to the desk of Detective Peter Vatterott.

The short, bullish cop had maybe ten years on Joe, and it showed in the thickening waist, thinning brown hair. The permanent squint in his hazel eyes suggested chronic suspicion.

"What's your interest in the case, Riley?" he asked.

"I've just learned of Monica Abrigado's death. I've been out of the country on assignment and didn't know. We'd been…ah…dating."

The cop's eyes had drifted to the monitor of his computer. "Hmm. Long assignment." He turned back to Joe.

"Exactly when did you leave the country?"

Joe named the date and added the name of his company. Vatterott glanced back at the screen and then made a note on the blotter on his desk.

"It was practically open and shut," he said, returning his attention to Joe.

"It looked like a professional hit right from the beginning. We'd been keeping an eye on the Kismet Club for a while, and she was found in the alley behind it. But we didn't have enough evidence for an arrest. Less than a week later we learned that transfer of ownership had been made to a Jersey capo and that Don Springer, the original owner, was being kept on as manger." He shook his head. "Curious, to say the least. But nothing we could take to court."

"What happened to the roommate?"

Vatterott pressed some keys and refreshed his memory with the aid of the information on the computer screen.

"That was another story. In the initial investigation, the roomie—" he leaned forward, squinting at the screen "—Katelynn Adams...was on our suspect list, disappearing the way she did. Or at least a material witness."

He scratched his head and fumbled in his pockets as though searching for a cigarette. He gave up and settled instead for a sip of cola from the can on his desk.

"We put an APB out on Adams, but before we could initiate an all-state, we found the shooter."

"How did that happen?"

The older man shrugged. "Guy was gunned down during an attempted holdup. Liquor store. Turned out ballistics on the gun he used for the holdup matched the Abrigado shoot.

"We canceled the APB right then. Case closed as far as we were concerned. No need to spend man hours or money looking for Adams."

"Why was there a hit on Monica?"

The detective shrugged. "Never found that out. The shooter was dead, couldn't answer questions. Obviously she pissed off the wrong people."

"What about her children, the twin babies?"

Vatterott nodded. "Yeah. Well, the first uniform at the scene found the phone dangling off the hook at the pay phone at the corner. A trace showed the last call was made to the apartment Abrigado shared with Adams. Abrigado's prints were on the handset. We pieced together that she'd called to warn Adams and told her to get the kids out of there. That eliminated kidnapping on Adams's part. By the time we got to the apartment the place had been trashed—probably by the mob—which supported our case. Abrigado had no family of record, nobody to come forward and claim the kids.

Obviously she trusted the roomie since she was the baby-sitter on record when Abrigado worked at night.''

Vatterott wound down and stood up, indicating the interview was over as far as he was concerned.

Joe got to his feet as well, but he had one last question. ''What about the father?''

Vatterott shook his head. ''Never turned up in our investigation, probably because we closed the case so quick.''

Joe felt angry. ''Nice for you guys that you got all the answers you needed without spending too much time or money on the case, but it sure feels like the whole thing—especially the missing kids and roomie—was swept under the rug.''

The other man shrugged. ''You wanna see numbers on the city's crime logs?'' He gestured around the room, drawing Joe's attention to the crowded desks, with cops hunched at every one, phones ringing non-stop, people rushing in and out.

''This is a light day, which is why I had time to talk to you. You figure it out.''

He gestured at the door. ''I'll walk you down. I could use a smoke.''

Suddenly he stopped. ''Wait a minute, Riley.''

He dashed back to his desk and pawed through a drawer. He found what he was looking for and held it out as he rejoined Joe.

Joe took the card. Matt Wilkins, Private Investigations, the card read. There was an address and phone number in the lower right corner.

''If it's important to you, this guy can probably get you more answers. Got a pretty good track record.''

''Thanks.'' Joe pocketed the card.

They shook hands on the steps of the precinct house.

The detective squinted at Joe. "You might want to check out city hall. If those babies were born here, there'll be a record. Maybe the birth father is named."

THE BIRTH RECORD LISTED the father as "unknown."

Joe thought maybe he should drop the whole thing and get on with his vacation and the business of looking for an apartment.

But by the time he'd finished his lunch at the counter of the coffee shop near his hotel, he realized he wasn't going to be able to let it go.

He called the Wilkins agency from the pay phone on the street and was told Wilkins could see him immediately.

He walked the ten blocks and arrived just as Matt Wilkins was finishing his own lunch at his desk.

Tall, rangy, with a handlebar mustache, Matt Wilkins could have been a sheriff out of the Old West. Joe thought he even detected a Western twang in the man's accent.

"Nice of Vatterott to think of me," Wilkins said, handing the card back to Joe. "Now, why don't you sit down and tell me how I can help you."

Joe repeated what the super and the homicide detective had told him.

Wilkins was a good listener, neither interrupting nor moving while Joe spoke.

"You think the kids—the twins—are yours" was his first comment when Joe finished.

Until that moment, Joe hadn't been aware himself that that was a possibility, though the date of the twins' birth would have been right.

He cleared his throat and shrugged. "If they were

mine, why wouldn't Monica have named me on the birth certificate?''

Wilkins smiled. ''Maybe she wasn't monogamous, didn't know for sure who the daddy was.''

''I guess that's a possibility,'' he said. ''But if the kids are mine, I want to know it. They've got tests for that sort of thing, don't they?''

''Yeah, they sure do. But first you'd have to find the kids.''

''Well, I guess that's why I'm here.'' Suddenly he felt better, felt as if he had a purpose, knew where he was going with this. ''You think you could find this Katelynn Adams, find the kids? And maybe find out more about why Monica was killed? If it was a hit, maybe you could find out who called it.''

Wilkins reached into a side drawer and pulled out a form. ''You got money?'' he asked as he rolled the form into a typewriter beside his desk. ''This ain't gonna be cheap.''

Joe pulled his checkbook out of his inside jacket pocket and threw it on the desk. ''I'm no millionaire, but I think I can handle the tab if you're on the square.''

Wilkins had his hands poised over the keyboard. He grimaced and nodded. ''All I'm lookin' for is enough to bring my secretary back to work.'' He peered up at Joe. ''You understand I can't give any guarantees.''

''But you'll do your best. Right?''

Wilkins turned back to the typewriter. ''You got it, Riley. Now, let's start with statistics.''

Three days later, Wilkins called to say that he had a preliminary report and Joe suggested they meet in the bar of his hotel.

He had been preoccupied with looking for an apartment and was both exhausted and frustrated by the futility of that.

"I don't understand why you want such a big apartment, Mr. Riley," the Realtor had commented. "After all, you're single, no kids, no family, and you say you aren't going to be looking for a roommate. I should think that one-bedroom we looked at in the Village would be perfect for you."

He hadn't been able to explain to the Realtor why he felt he needed more space. He didn't understand it himself. But everything he'd looked at was either too small or, if large enough, too pricey. And all the while she was showing him apartments, he found himself thinking of houses—trees, grass, gardens— a totally unrealistic vision for a man planning to settle in Manhattan for the next few years.

When he made the appointment with Wilkins, he was grateful for the distraction and eager to learn what Wilkins had discovered.

They ordered drinks and chatted casually as they took their first sips, and then Wilkins took a file folder out of his briefcase and set it on the table.

"You can read this later, but I'll give you the gist of what's here. First, regarding Monica Abrigado, I spoke to the employees at the Kismet Club. There were only a couple who were there when she was an employee. Springer, the manager, was out of town the day I was there, and I plan to see him when he gets back. The people I saw didn't have much to contribute. Seems all they recall is that she'd been having a thing with the boss and then she was killed. They all insisted that the two things weren't connected."

He took another swallow of his drink and rifled through the pages of his report.

"Then I started tracking Adams. I went out to Yonkers. Her last known place of employment before the murder was Hudson River Excursions, a paddlewheeler cruise company. She was a bookkeeper-cruise coordinator there until the place was shut down by the IRS. They were suspected of tax evasion and money laundering."

"So, the owners are in jail?"

Wilkins shook his head. "Apparently the IRS could never make their charges stick. The case was dropped and Henry Rotterman and Bill Hagar, the owners, reopened the business a couple of months later. By then, Adams had done her disappearing act and there was no question of hiring her back."

"You spoke with these guys…Rotterman and Hagar?"

"Yup. They appeared to be confused by my interest in Adams after all this time. Hagar was almost hostile and Rotterman seemed nervous as hell. But the bottom line was that they had no idea where she might have gone and knew nothing about the Abrigado murder or Adams's connection to her. I asked to talk with any of the Adams's co-workers who might have been close to her, but they insisted there was nobody around who'd worked there back then."

Joe heaved a sigh of disappointment and signaled to the waiter for another round.

"So, that's that, eh?"

"Not hardly," Wilkins said. "That was just preliminary stuff—looking for the obvious. Now that's out of the way, I start digging in earnest."

He sipped from his fresh drink and shook his head. "You know, these two, Rotterman and Hagar, struck me as a really sleazy pair. I'd bet my last dollar they were guilty as hell of those charges. But I think they were telling it straight when they denied knowing anything about where Adams had gone. I asked if they could come up with the names of some of her co-workers from back then and they promised to look up the information and get back to me. She'd worked there for years. It's unlikely she didn't get close to someone she worked with. Close enough to mention favorite places she's been or places she'd like to go. That sort of thing.''

"It would have been easier to find her right after the murder, if the cops had done their job,'' Joe snapped, and then regretted his show of temper. Detective Vatterott had justified the decisions made in the case at the time. They didn't have the vested interest that Joe himself had.

"So what next?'' he asked Wilkins.

"I've been thinking about the kids. They'd be about what—six years old now, right?''

"Yeah. Exactly.'' Joe tried to visualize six-year-old kids, but his frame of reference was sorely limited.

"So what do six-year-olds do?''

"Do?'' Joe shrugged. "I don't know. Go to school, maybe?''

Wilkins nodded, his face slight with satisfaction. "Exactly. So, that's where we start. Schools have records. I talked to a friend of mine who's a teacher. She said birth records are required to enroll a child in any school in New York State.''

"You think Adams stayed in the state?''

"I don't know. But it's logical to start with that assumption. Cheaper, too,'' he added with a wry grin.

"And if she went out of state?''

Wilkins shrugged. "That makes the job harder, but

why look for snags before we need to?'' He finished his drink, snapped the lock on his briefcase and stood up, holding his hand out to Joe.

''I'll be in touch.''

Joe browsed through the folder after Wilkins had gone. It was more in-depth, but the detective had touched on all the salient points.

Still no clues as to the motivation behind Monica's murder and nothing to point at the direction in which Adams had gone. It was as if she'd fallen off the face of the earth. But he knew that was a fanciful thought. A person, alone, might just disappear without a trace, get swallowed up in the huge dimensions of the country. But not a person toting two babies. There were so many complications with babies. Special furniture was needed for them, diapers, baby bottles and baby food. And as Wilkins had pointed out, eventually, school and school records.

By the time he'd paid the bill and returned to his room, he was feeling a good deal more optimistic. Wilkins was on the case and he trusted the guy. He had a good feeling about the case. Wilkins would find Katelynn Adams. And the children. The twins. A surge of excitement rose in his chest. *His children?*

WILKINS CALLED the next day.

''Are you sitting down, Riley?''

Joe collapsed on the side of the bed, his breath whooshing out of him on a gust of elation.

''Go'' was all he could manage.

''Someone named Monica Abrigado is alive and living in Lake George, New York!''

Chapter Two

The two women sat in their usual window booth at the Rainbow Café, huddled over cups of coffee and a plate containing the crumbs of Danish pastry. Their laughter rang out periodically, causing the other customers and café employees to look over and smile.

Now their conversation had become serious.

"Kate, it's more than five years since you came here, don't you think it's safe now? If anyone was still looking for you, they'd have shown up by now." Marybeth Simpson brushed her ash-blond hair back as she leaned across the table, her voice low and careful.

The tall, elegant red-haired woman shook her head. "I don't know, Marybeth. I don't think I'm ever going to feel completely safe. Not when I'm using someone else's name, and especially now that the kids are old enough to start asking questions. How are they going to deal with the fact that their whole life was based on lies?"

"Damn it," Marybeth whispered, leaning closer and clutching Kate's hand on the tabletop, "they're going to be grateful to you for protecting them, for giving them nothing but love and care their whole lives. You've been the best mother any kid could ask for, and unless they turn out to be the most selfish, insensitive two people in the world, they're going to acknowledge all you've done for them and love you for it.''

Kate turned her hand in Marybeth's and squeezed her to show appreciation for her best friend's support. She'd never regretted telling Marybeth Simpson the whole story, and there were so many times she'd needed to be able to talk about the past to hear the other woman's assurances for the future.

"I know you're right, and I probably overreacted when Sam started pressuring me for answers. It was like the Inquisition, and it seemed like every answer I gave him created a new question I couldn't answer. It didn't help after I'd had the feeling of being followed all day."

"Okay," Marybeth said, slumping back in her seat and pushing her wire-rimmed glasses back up her nose, "so you dated Sam, who was definitely a jerk and didn't know when to back off. But that's no excuse for you to go back into hiding, Kate. No reason for you to stop dating."

"I'm not hiding, Marybeth! I wish you'd quit calling it that. I'm just…careful."

"Careful's good," Marybeth said, trying to keep a straight face, "but horny's better."

Kate had to laugh, partly in relief that her friend had so effectively changed the subject and lightened the mood.

"You're so bad, Marybeth. I'm just glad the parents of your charges don't see the real you, or they'd never leave their little darlings in your care. I even wonder why I…"

Her words trailed away as she noticed that Marybeth

was no longer laughing and was staring, mesmerized, out of the window.

"What are you looking at?" She turned her head to follow her friend's rapt gaze.

A man was coming up the sidewalk alongside the window of the café. He was a tall, lean man, with broad shoulders, brown hair that glinted gold highlights in the sunlight and a square jaw with a cleft chin.

A sigh caught in Kate's throat as her eyes met and held the deep gray gaze of the man as he turned his head toward her. She barely registered the low moan that Marybeth emitted. For herself she seemed almost caught in a vacuum in which no sound or sight existed except for the sight of the man's face, the sound of her own heart pounding in her chest. A sense of familiarity washed over her, making her want to reach out, to touch that face. She lifted her hand to the pane. The cool, hard feel of the glass restored her to her senses just as the man pulled his gaze from hers and turned his head.

"Now, that's any woman's type," Marybeth gasped.

Kate swallowed. What a strange reaction to a perfect stranger. She had never been the kind of woman to get caught up in physical attraction, and certainly not over what had amounted to a mere second in passing.

"Tourist," she muttered, reaching for her coffee cup. "Pull yourself together, Simpson, tourists are off limits."

"Ooh, but that one was worth breaking the rules for. Admit it, Kate."

Kate shook her head and grinned. "How about the rules pertaining to adultery, dear friend?"

"Details, details," Marybeth said, her voice still rapturous. But Kate noticed her friend was twisting the wedding band on her left hand.

"Come on, I'm due at the office in five." She snatched up the bill and slid out of the booth.

They parted company in front of the café. "See you later," Kate said. "Give my brats an extra hug from me and tell them I'll pick them up at three for the game."

"Done," Marybeth said, hitching her shoulder bag back up and turning away. She stopped and turned back. "Kate, did that guy look familiar to you?"

Had her friend read her mind? "Tourists. They all look alike after a while," she said, pretending an insouciance she didn't feel.

"Well, maybe it's time to forget the rule about not dating tourists," Marybeth said, a mischievous grin lighting up her face. "Better a temporary fling than never getting flung at all."

Kate was still chuckling when she came to the low brick building that housed Lake George Paddlewheel Tours. She sobered as she looked up and down the street before unlocking the door, a habit of long-standing. But Marybeth was right. After five years, it was unlikely that anyone would still be looking for her.

If only she could shake the feeling of being followed.

"Get over yourself, Katie," she muttered. "The world doesn't revolve around you."

She let herself into the building and was greeted by the ringing phone. Gratefully she took a breath and launched into her professional persona.

JOE RILEY HADN'T EXPECTED to see the woman right there in the window of the café as he passed it. When she made eye contact with him, he'd felt his stomach lurch with excitement. Only a foot of space separated them. That and the plate glass of the window. She was even more beautiful up close like that.

She had jade-green eyes that seemed to look right into the depths of his soul. Did she recognize him, realize he'd had her under surveillance for the last couple of days? No, that hadn't been a look of fear, or even recognition. It was more like a kind of spiritual connection. Recognition at a deeper level than spotting someone you'd seen before.

Now he hung back in the shadows of the interior of the Bait & Boat Shop, watching as she entered the building across the street. The furtive way she'd checked the street first reminded him of his own mission and what she was really all about.

"Help you, sir?" a voice asked behind him.

Joe, startled out of his reverie, jerked around. "Uh…thanks. I just wanted a map of the lakes region, if you carry them."

The clerk went to a rack on the wall behind the desk.

"Planning on doing a little fishing?"

Joe saw an opening and went for it. "Maybe. Mostly I've been thinking about hiring a boat and touring the lakes region."

"We rent boats," the clerk said, coming around the desk with a couple of maps.

Joe nodded. "Yeah, I saw your sign." He accepted the maps and tilted his head toward the front window. "Speaking of boats, looks like they've got a pretty good excursion business going across the street."

"Yup. Seems like the last few years the place just took off. Gal that manages it is a right go-getter. Came up with some fancy ideas and about doubled what they used to do." He shook his head. "Can't get used to so many women in business, but that one sure seems to know her stuff."

Joe pretended to be studying a display of fishing rods.

"She from around here?"

"Nope. Been here about five years or so. Got lucky because the owner was wanting to retire and was going to sell. She talked him into keeping the business and hiring her to run it for him. Worked out good. For both of 'em."

"Must have had some experience in that business, eh?"

The older man shook his head. "Can't say. She's not one to talk about herself much and I'm not one to pry. All I know is she's been good for that business and sent plenty my way as well."

"Married?"

The man had been tidying the boxes of lures in a glass case as he spoke. He stopped now and looked up at Joe, his eyes glinting with suspicion.

"You got a personal interest?"

Joe realized he'd gone too far, that the man wasn't going to idly gossip about his neighbor.

He shrugged and managed a sheepish expression. "Just nosy. It's the nature of the beast, I guess," he said, throwing out the first cliché that came to mind.

"And what beast would that be?"

"I...um...I'm a journalist."

"Hmm. Well, won't find much to report on around here. We're mostly a small town when tourist season is over. Not much crime and not much of interest to anyone but us."

It sounded like a suggestion to butt out. Joe knew when to pull back. He paid for the maps.

"Come on back when you decide about that boat rental," the clerk said, ringing up the purchase on an old-fashioned register. "Got just about any kind of craft you might be interested in."

Joe agreed and left the store. Beyond the building across the street, he could see the MV *Georgia* docked at the landing, her flags flying, paint glistening in the sunshine, crew scurrying around both decks preparing for business.

Should he confront her now or wait until the boat left the dock and he could be sure she'd be alone in the office?

Fresh excitement assaulted him. Nerves. And he hadn't had breakfast. Maybe he'd take care of that first. She probably wouldn't be leaving the building again during the morning hours.

He walked back to the Rainbow Café, took the very seat his quarry had vacated in the window booth and ordered breakfast.

Sipping coffee, he stared out of the window and let his mind drift back over the past couple of days.

First had come Wilkins's shocking bit of news. Joe had protested. He'd seen the police report; Monica's body had been positively ID'd by fingerprints that matched the fingerprints on her cabaret license.

But Wilkins had substantiated his claim. Ashleigh Morgan Abrigado and Robert Lee Abrigado, fraternal twins, were enrolled in Lake George Elementary School last year as kindergartners. They would be entering first grade there in the fall.

Listed as parent-guardian: Monica Katherine Abrigado.

After much discussion, they'd agreed that Joe would be the one to go to Lake George and check it out. He had known Monica; would recognize her even if she'd assumed some kind of disguise. Assuming the cops had made a mistake and it wasn't Monica whose body had been found in that alley.

On his first day in Lake George, overcast skies and a light drizzle had turned the world wet and gray. Joe had parked up the street from the address Wilkins had given him and watched, through the moving windshield wipers, as the tall redhead had emerged from the house with the children. A tightening in his chest made him gasp for breath at the first sighting of the kids. They were gorgeous, with lustrous dark hair and big, bright eyes, the color of which he couldn't determine from that distance. Their bodies were lean and athletic. They seemed tall for six-year-olds, though he'd been forced to admit that he didn't really know what the norm was.

Robert and Ashleigh. He whispered the names aloud and pangs of loneliness pierced him. What if they were his? His son, his daughter, the fact of them kept from him all these years? He could feel his pulse racing as he visualized them learning he was their father. He shook his head and uttered an expletive under his breath. There was no proof they were his, and he was setting himself up for trouble if he jumped the gun on this.

He turned his attention to the woman. The woman definitely wasn't Monica. Monica had been short, voluptuous, dark and sultry. Hair dye and contact lenses wouldn't have been enough to account for the discrepancies.

He'd followed from a three-car distance and watched as she dropped the kids at a day-care center with the cutesy name, Kiddy Korner. Another woman, a petite, bespectacled blonde, had come out and greeted them. Hugs were exchanged and the twins ran into the building while the two women stood and spoke for a few minutes. When the redhead returned to her Honda, he followed her to the Rainbow Café, but before he could decide whether to park and wait, she came out with a paper bag and drove on to the Lake George Excursion Tours Company.

She'd stayed in the building until four o'clock, when she'd locked up, got in her car and gone back to Kiddy Korner to pick up the children. Joe had watched from his car as lights went on in various rooms in the house and the threesome seemed to settle in for the evening.

He'd returned to his motel and called Wilkins later to share his findings.

"It's got to be the baby-sitter, Katelynn Adams. It isn't Monica."

Wilkins's sigh of relief was audible. "Well, that's one complication that's out of the way. So, did you approach her, talk to her?"

"No. I…" Joe hesitated, unable to express the flood of emotions that had overwhelmed him at the sight of the children. "I thought I'd do a little nosing around first."

"Yeah, maybe that's a good idea. You know, my first thought was that Adams would have unloaded the kids on someone else. But it's got to be her. Nobody else would be using Abrigado's name. Interesting that she's kept them all these years."

"Oh, she kept them all right," Joe said. "They're a regular little family, from the looks of things."

"Well, let me know what goes down after you talk

to her, and meanwhile, I'm still working on the other angle of the case. Be in touch.''

Her routine this day had differed only in that this time, with the sun shining and a soft breeze drying the streets, the woman and the twins had walked to Kiddy Korner. Then, after the kids had gone inside, the blond woman had joined Adams, and they'd walked the few blocks toward the center of town.

Joe couldn't very well keep following them in a car; the slower pace would have made him stand out. So he'd driven by them, parked near the excursion company and strolled idly back toward the business district. Strolled right by this café where he'd made eye contact with the woman.

The waitress interrupted his reverie. He smiled and thanked her as she set his eggs down in front of him. The eggs were done the way he liked, the bacon and toast crisp, the coffee hot and strong, but Joe hardly noticed what he ate as his mind took him through various scenarios in which he would confront Katelynn Adams.

He still hadn't settled on a firm plan when he finished his breakfast and walked back out onto the street. It was only 10:00 a.m. and the streets were beginning to fill with tourists on foot or in cars. If Adams had a firm routine, she wouldn't be leaving her office much before four o'clock.

By the time he got back in his car, he realized that the stress of the drive yesterday, and the day spent trailing the woman, had taken its toll on him. He was still suffering the time difference since the arrival from Saudi Arabia and the drag of too much leisure time after years of intense work schedules. He could grab a nap back at his motel for a couple of hours and still have plenty of time to catch up with Katelynn Adams before she left work.

He slept until two-thirty and woke feeling more tired than when he'd lain down. He decided a big dose of fresh air was called for, and given that Adams was on foot today, he left the car in the motel lot and walked back to town.

He had hoped to find her alone in her office, but she was already locking up when he strolled around the corner at the end of the block on which her building was located. He hung back and then followed a few minutes later. Easy to keep her in sight with that bright red hair blazing in the sunlight. He stayed back a block, matching his pace to hers.

She picked up the children, and then, instead of heading toward home, they went in the opposite direction.

Two blocks from Kiddy Korner they entered a park and the children ran ahead toward the baseball field.

Joe waited until Adams had settled with a group of other women on the front bench and then took a seat up in the back of the bleachers.

He watched as the coach fitted padded vests on both the children and a catcher's mask on Robbie. When he propped baseball hats on their heads, the twins simultaneously turned the bills to the back, causing Joe to chuckle. When Ashleigh marched out to the pitcher's mound, Joe felt as if his chest were going to burst with pride. How many girls were pitchers? She must be really good.

He was caught up in the game immediately, though it was more of a practice session with the coach frequently interrupting to run out and explain things to the players. When Robbie yelled something at Ashleigh and she threw down her mitt and marched up to her brother, hands on hips, chin thrust out, Joe laughed out loud. The kid's stance said it all. She wasn't taking any lip from anyone, not even her own twin. His amusement turned to alarm when the twins rounded off, fists at the ready. The coach intervened before they could come to blows and Joe slumped, relieved, back on his seat.

After half an hour, the kids changed positions and the twins came up to bat. When Robbie hit a home run, Joe jumped to his feet to cheer and noticed that the Adams woman was standing on her seat yelling louder than anyone, her arms raised in triumph.

She might have kidnapped the kids, maybe even had something to do with the death of their mother, but it was obvious she had real maternal feelings for them. Joe couldn't help but wonder how she was going to take it if and when the twins were taken from her. How were the kids going to take it? His stomach plummeted at the thought. The breaking up of a family, even one founded on lies, seemed horrendous, and the fact that he might be the cause of it threw him for a loop. For a moment he considered backing away, just getting in his rental car and driving back to Manhattan and dropping the whole thing.

But then the game was over, the kids pairing up with their parents, and over the voices of kids and grown-ups, Joe heard Ashleigh call out, "I call front seat, Mommy."

Mommy! The term, uttered in the child's innocent voice, made him mad all over again. He wasn't going anywhere until he learned the truth, and if that upset anyone, including the kids, too bad! That was life—

nobody ever said it was going to be all sunshine and happy endings.

EARLY THE NEXT MORNING, Kate was poring over the accounts. She looked up from the figures in the ledger and smiled automatically.

"Hi, can I help you?" Her smile faded as she recognized the man standing in the doorway.

He seemed to fill the room, his presence as overwhelming as his size. Not a small woman herself, Kate was amazed at the way he made her feel frail and helpless. In self-defense she stood up. It helped only marginally.

"You can if you're the manager."

She nodded.

"Well, I was interested in checking out your boat tours."

Kate stifled a sigh of relief. What had she expected? She'd already pegged the man as a tourist. So why the sense of...danger? No, too strong a word. Not danger, but definitely trouble.

She forced herself to focus on the reality of the situation. She came out from around her desk, her hand thrust out in greeting.

"I'm Monica Abrigado."

He took her hand and looked into her eyes, his gaze penetrating.

"Monica Abrigado?"

"I...yes. Is there something wrong with my name?"

He shook his head, kept her eyes locked with him, her hand clasped in his. "You don't look like a Monica for some reason."

She flushed. "My middle name is Katherine. My friends call me Kate."

He nodded. "Makes sense." He let go of her hand and looked around the room, as if he'd suddenly lost interest in her.

"I can show you our brochures, Mr...."

"Riley. Joe Riley." He hesitated, seemed to expect a response.

Kate didn't have one. She shrugged.

The man seemed to come to a decision. "Yeah, brochures would be good."

Kate returned to her chair and opened a side drawer from which she withdrew a folder. When she saw that he was still standing across the room, she gestured him to the chair opposite hers.

He took the brochure and began to shuffle through them.

"Are you interested in a charter cruise, Mr. Riley?"

"I...um...maybe. What would that involve?"

"Well, that would depend on your company's requirements," Kate said, frowning.

"Company? Oh, right. Well...um...how about you give me a rundown."

"Certainly." Kate sat back, her hands steepled on the desk. "If yours is a large company party, we'd use the *Georgia.* She holds five hundred and carries a full crew, caterers and a dance band for private charters. The *Mermaid* is a smaller paddlewheel and can only accommodate parties up to a hundred and fifty. We use her for the daily excursions as a general rule unless she's been chartered for a private affair. The cost of the charter is based on which of the boats you need, number of hours you'd wish to be out, and whether you'd want food and music. We also have special features such as casino equipment, circus paraphernalia…special party motifs, you know. Those cost extra, of course.''

Joe Riley looked confused.

Kate softened. ''Never coordinated a company party before, Mr. Riley?''

''You've found me out,'' he admitted, grinning. The grin caused her stomach to do somersaults.

''Ever been on a paddlewheeler before?'' she asked.

''No.''

''Well, listen, I've an idea.'' She lifted a glossy sheet out from the brochures in front of him and placed it on top.

''We're starting the first of the season's daily excursion runs tomorrow. Why don't you come aboard, as my guest, and get a feel for what a cruise would be like. Maybe after you've been aboard, you'll decide that a boat is not the best place for your company party. I'd hate to lose the business, but I prefer you don't regret your decision after the fact.''

The picture showed the MV *Mermaid* with Lake George sparkling in the background. The printing below announced the maiden voyage and named the future days and times of the public excursions with the price in smaller print. Also listed were the amenities offered on the cruises: sandwich-lunch boxes, drinks, ice cream, candy and cigarettes.

''Will you be aboard?''

Kate had planned a picnic with the children on Sunday. Suddenly a picnic aboard the *Mermaid* seemed more enticing. The children would love it.

''Yes, as a matter of fact, I will.'' She swiveled in her chair, lifted a roll of tickets out of a box on the shelf behind her desk and tore one off.

''Here. You'll need this to get aboard.'' She stood

up. "I'll look forward to seeing you tomorrow, Mr. Riley, and I'm sure you'll see for yourself how well a boat would work for your company party."

Only after he'd left her office did Kate slump back in her seat, heaving an enormous sigh of relief.

She'd been running this business for five years; she'd be at a loss to figure out how many male customers she'd met in that time. None had ever had such an immediate—and terrifying—effect on her.

And again there was that sense of familiarity; she'd experienced it when she looked into his eyes, when he grinned, when his face tinged slightly with embarrassment over his lack of experience at planning a party.

But of course they had never met before. It must be that he reminded her of someone else she had met somewhere in her past and that was all there was to that.

She picked up the brochures and put them back in the envelope. The placard of the *Mermaid* public excursion trembled in her hand as she thought about seeing Joe Riley again the next day.

JOE TOOK A DEEP BREATH and leaned against the piling on the wharf. He'd meant to confront her, come right out and tell her he knew who she was, knew she had stolen Monica's identity, knew she was passing herself off as the twins' mother. And then he'd meant to hit her with the news that he was most likely the children's father and intended...

What? To claim them? Take them away from here, away from her? Take them where? He hadn't even managed to find an apartment. It struck him then that he'd actually been looking for an apartment that could accommodate the children as well as himself. Subconsciously that had been his reason for turning down all those perfectly adequate one-bedroom apartments the Realtor had shown him.

"And then what?" he muttered aloud. "What do I know about raising kids?"

A couple of fishermen passed by on the pier and gave him a cautious look. He turned away, facing out to the water.

The whole thing had an insane feeling to it, and just to prove it, he was even talking to himself now.

Matt Wilkins. The detective had a way of getting to the bottom line. Joe needed a dose of that kind of calm, sane thinking. He headed back to the motel to call the man.

Chapter Three

"You have to admit this is a very clever woman," Matt said. "She must have been long-sighted to work it out that one day the children would have to be enrolled in school and that she'd need their birth certificates. Which means using their real names. She figures that Monica's dead, nobody's going to be looking for her anymore, so it's safe to assume her name, whereas they might still be looking for Katelynn Adams. Very clever."

"And very dishonest," Joe snapped.

"Maybe you're coming at this from the wrong angle, Joe. Why not consider the possibility that her motives were all good? She did what Monica asked her to do—spirited the kids away to a safe place. Then she learns of Monica's death. She's scared. She's thinking, what if the people who killed Monica come looking for her and the kids? Maybe her first priority is protecting those little babies. Look at it that way, and you gotta figure the woman's sacrificed her own life—her very identity—to give the kids a chance."

Joe stopped his pacing and carried the phone back to the bed, where he slumped on the side of the mattress. He hadn't looked at it from this angle.

"Well, I wanted the voice of reason, Matt. I guess I got it."

"Don't beat yourself up, Joe. My scenario is just that—another viewpoint. Only Adams herself knows the truth. So maybe that's the place to start. You go to that thing tomorrow, spend a little time with her, do a little careful investigating, get a feel for where she's coming from. Just keep in mind that a good investigator doesn't go in with preconceived ideas but keeps an open mind."

Joe agreed. "Anything new at your end?"

"I'm going to meet with Don Springer tomorrow. After that, I'm going back out to Yonkers, see if the guys from HRE came up with that list of past employees so I can talk to them."

"Why bother? We've got Adams now."

"Just clearing up loose ends," Wilkins said. "See if there's anything anyone knows that we missed. Just a feeling, you know. Lots of answers come from following the old hunch. Besides, I'm not working on any other cases right now, so I have plenty of time and it's best to be sure that Adams is in no way connected to Abrigado's death, isn't it? I think you need that bottom line, don't you, Joe?"

Joe could see the rationale in that.

They agreed to be in touch when either of them had anything to report, and Joe hung up feeling marginally better.

He put on a clean shirt, a tie and lightweight linen jacket and walked down to the motel dining room, where he took a table by the window overlooking the lake and ordered dinner.

While he waited he thought about Katelynn Adams. Kate. The name suited her. Irish-sounding to match that red hair and those green eyes. She was more slender, taller than the women he'd been drawn to in the past, but for that matter, he'd never been so immediately drawn by any woman he'd known. It occurred to him that every relationship he'd ever had had started out in a most casual, tentative way and continued in the same vein right to the end. If he were to describe his previous involvements with women he'd have to characterize them more as friendships with sex thrown in almost as an afterthought. Plenty of physical passion but very little emotional passion.

He cut into the steak the waiter had served him and chewed thoughtfully. What did that say about him as a man? Was he passionless by nature? He'd always assumed things would change when he met the "right" woman. There was a certain irony in the fact that though Monica might have borne his children, even she hadn't qualified as "right."

A glint of light caught his attention peripherally. He turned his head and saw the huge bulk of the MV *Georgia* making its lumbersome way through the twilit evening. Though the interior cabins on both decks were well lit, he saw no sign of passengers. Perhaps the pilot had only taken it out on a test run. Joe knew the season was just beginning, that a test run was a likely scenario.

He put his fork down and watched the boat, imagining himself aboard the vessel, Kate beside him at the rail on the upper deck. There'd be a moon casting its light on the backwash churned up by the paddlewheel. *And moonlight setting her red hair ablaze.*

Almost guiltily Joe looked around the dining room. Nobody was paying particular attention to him, and in any case nobody could read his mind. He thought about what Matt had said. If he'd been unfair in his judgment of Kate, would that make a difference in the way he would explain his presence in Lake George, in her life?

And how would she take it?

The thought made his stomach tighten. He sipped from his beer glass, the coolness in his throat becoming warmth when it reached his stomach. It soothed the spasm.

He resumed eating and contemplated a different approach. He'd take his time, get to know her, ask subtle questions, make no immediate declarations. If it turned out that her motives had been entirely innocent, it would behoove him to win her friendship before he laid the explosive truth at her feet.

But a part of him hoped she'd turn out to be guilty of something so that he wouldn't have to watch that happy sparkle in her green eyes fade out to be replaced by dull disillusionment.

KATE COULDN'T HAVE ASKED for a more perfect day for the first excursion if she'd had a direct line to God, she thought as she swept the twins ahead of her up the gangplank. The sky was a cloud-free cover of cerulean, and the breeze that blew hinted of warming temperatures as the day wore on.

"Mom, can we stand at the rail and watch people come aboard, and then can we go up to the pilot's cabin?" Robbie begged, jumping up and down with excitement.

"First things first, honey," Kate warned. "We'll pick a table in the cabin and leave our jackets there to hold our places, and then we can—"

"I want to go down to the engine room," Ashleigh protested. "Why do we always have to do what he wants first?"

Kate groaned inwardly. Was it going to be one of "those" kinds of days, where the twins disagreed on absolutely everything? Maybe the weather was the only perfection the day would hold.

But just then she spotted Joe Riley coming up the gangplank, and even as her stomach plummeted, her spirits soared.

"Before we do anything, there's someone I want you kids to meet," she said, automatically reaching up to tidy the breeze-blown curls that wisped along her cheek. She straightened the collar of her mint-green gingham blouse and the waistband of her white jeans, then silently berated herself for being so nervous.

"We already know everybody," Ashleigh said. "I don't want to meet anyone else." She started for the rail, Robbie in close pursuit.

Kate had a firm hold on the collars of each of the kids' shirts when Joe joined them.

"Looks like you've got your hands full," he said, grinning at her obvious discomfort.

"Leashes are against the law in New York State," Kate said, irritated by the man's levity at her expense. She wondered if he was one of those men who thought he could raise children better than a woman. Especially when he was never going to be tested.

Joe squatted down in front of Ashleigh and held out his hand. "Joe Riley. Pleased to meet you, Ms. Abrigado."

Ashleigh, suddenly shy, turned her face against Kate's hip.

"Ash don't wanta meet no one today," her brother explained. "But I'm Robbie, I'll meetcha." He stuck out his hand.

Joe studied the streaks of chocolate on the kid's palm

and then grasped it in a firm grip, trying not to cringe at the feel.

Kate hid a grin and turned toward the door of the cabin. "We should get a table before the mob takes over," she said, moving the children forward.

The tables were lined along the walls so that each had a view of the lake, and each was covered with a red cloth with gold fringe that matched the café curtains at the windows. There was a bar along the back bulkhead where refreshments were sold, and Joe saw that the bartender had garters on the sleeves of his long-sleeved white shirt, the way they had on old riverboats.

Joe took out his wallet. "I sure am thirsty," he said, looking at no one in particular. "I could sure go for a cola if there was someone to get it."

Ashleigh, her shyness overcome at the prospect of treats, fairly leaped up in her chair beside Kate, yelling, "I'll go, I'll go." Robbie almost climbed into Joe's lap as he protested that he was the one who should get to go.

"Let's see," Joe said, "there're four of us. So, that would mean I'd need two people with two hands to go."

The twins exchanged a look, working out the math. "I've got two hands," they said at the same moment, nodding their heads in unison.

Joe laughed as they snatched the bills and ran the length of the cabin to the bar.

"So," he said, slouching back in his chair and smiling at Kate, "this is sort of a busman's holiday for you."

Kate shrugged and fiddled with the clasp on her leather purse. "I try not to let anything interfere with my Sundays with the kids, so I figured I'd kill two birds with one stone.''

Joe nodded. "And where's Mr....Abrigado?"

Kate tried to hold back the flush she felt tinting her cheeks, but it was an impossible task. She lowered her eyes and murmured, "He d-died."

"Aah...I see. So it's just you and the kids."

Kate nodded and lifted her gaze to meet his. "It's enough," she said, thrusting her chin forward to emphasize her words.

Joe lifted his hands in a gesture of surrender. "Okay, lady, don't shoot."

She laughed. God, he was so good-looking with those amazing gray eyes and that honey-blond hair. He was wearing khakis and a long-sleeved, beige knit shirt. It was collarless with three buttons at the throat. He'd left the buttons open, and she could see a sprinkling of blond chest hair. Casual, but somehow sexy on him. She blinked, startled by the direction her thoughts were taking.

She cleared her throat and resorted to her professional facade to hide her more personal interest.

"So, Mr. Riley, what do you do?"

"Do?"

"Your company, your job?"

Joe grabbed the last lie he'd told on the subject and repeated it. "I'm a freelance journalist," he said, pretending to watch the children's cautious return with the drinks.

"Oh. Well then, there is no company...to charter the boat, I mean."

Her confusion, and the questions it raised, was interrupted by the children's return.

"Mommy, they're selling tickets now. Can we go to the rail and watch?" Robbie begged.

Kate gave Joe a level look. "We'll get back to this," she warned.

They went to the rail and watched the passengers come aboard, waving at the local people they knew. Then Ashleigh insisted it was her turn to choose, and they went to the engine room where the noise of the pumps was deafening, though it didn't deter the little girl from shouting myriad questions.

The revelry on deck and in the cabin seemed quiet by contrast. Robbie began begging to go up to the pilot's cabin, but Kate insisted they had to eat lunch first. She made the twins promise to sit quietly with Mr. Riley while she went to the bar for sandwiches, and for once they heeded her request. She kept looking over her shoulder to check, and they seemed very wrapped up in conversation with the man. For a moment she felt a surge of panic, but then she reminded herself that the children knew nothing they might inadvertently give away. She still hadn't figured out why Riley had shown up at her office and let her think he was considering a charter, and she was determined to set that record straight as soon as possible. Meanwhile, it was probably safest to keep him in her sights. He couldn't mean any harm to them in such a public place.

When she returned to the table with four box lunches, she caught the tail end of their conversation.

"And we take swimming, too," Ashleigh was saying, "but I like baseball better and Robbie likes fishing best."

"Do not!" Robbie almost shouted.

"Do, too!" Ashleigh's chin forewarned imminent fisticuffs.

Kate leaped the last step and plunked the white cardboard boxes on the table between them.

"I like eating the best," she said, loudly enough to interrupt the confrontation.

Ashleigh slumped back in her chair and glared at Robbie. Joe looked up at Kate and tried to keep a straight face. "I'm with your mom. I think eating's more fun than anything."

"I don't like tuna fish," Ashleigh warned.

"I hate tuna fish," Robbie agreed.

"Who said anything about tuna fish?" Kate asked, avoiding Joe's eyes.

"I'm not crazy about tuna fish, either," Joe said, making his voice meek.

The twins stared at him and then burst into gales of laughter.

Kate sat down and put her arms around the boxes. "I don't think any of you want these lunches."

"But I'm hungry," Joe whined in a pretty good imitation of a six-year-old.

Robbie looked up at the man and back at his mother. "Me, too," he said, his eyes pleading.

"What if it's tuna fish?" Kate asked, keeping her voice firm with great effort.

"I ain't eating it," Ashleigh said defiantly, folding her arms across her chest.

"Well...I don't know...I'm pretty hungry," Joe said. "I could probably eat a horse."

"A horse!" The other passengers looked over at Ashleigh's screech and Robbie's hollered "yechs."

Kate glared at Joe. "How many grown-ups at this table, Riley?" she demanded over the din.

She shoved a box in front of each of the three of them and ignored the twins' exaggerated comments about how much they "just loved" ham and cheese sandwiches.

"What's this?" Joe asked, opening his own sandwich.

"Roast beef and swiss."

"How come I didn't get ham and cheese?" he asked, inciting the children to giggles around mouths full of sandwich.

"You struck me as a red meat man."

"Ham's red."

Kate's sigh expressed her exasperation. She shoved her box at him. "How about chicken salad?"

She reached for his box and got a slap on the hand for it, creating further delight in the twins.

By the time they'd settled down to eating, Kate had totally forgotten about Riley's apparent subterfuge, and after the meal, when the children were taken by one of the crew to visit the pilot, she fell into careful conversation with him.

He seemed very interested in the children, which both surprised and pleased her. She asked if he'd ever been married, had children. He said he had never been married. She took that to answer the question in full.

He asked if she was a native of Lake George. She said she wasn't and hurriedly changed the subject.

She asked him if he lived in New York. He said he did now. She asked where he'd lived before, and he told her he'd been out of the country for a while.

"On assignment?" she asked. He hesitated and then acknowledged that was so.

They were both relieved to see the young crew member pass the window with the twins in tow. The threesome stopped at the rail and Kate gathered up their jackets and suggested to Joe that they join them out on deck.

"Thanks, Billy," Kate said, glancing at her watch. "Almost time to dock, isn't it?"

"Guess so, Kate. I'd better start getting ready."

The young man moved toward the stern and Kate looked up at Joe.

"I hope the day wasn't too boring for you," she said politely.

"Hardly that. In fact, I was just thinking, it's only two o'clock...early yet...seems a shame to waste the rest of the day."

They were standing close enough for Kate to see the black rim around the gray irises of his eyes. He had a deep tan that didn't look artificially achieved and didn't look as if it would fade any time soon. The kind of skin a man would have who'd worked outdoors continually, and under a hot sun. His scent was tickling her nostrils; not the sweet aftershave most men used, but something cleaner with a slightly woodsy undertone. Up close like this, his size didn't seem as overwhelming as it did comforting.

Kate swallowed with difficulty.

"I...I don't..."

"Well, I was thinking maybe we could continue the party somewhere else. Like say...Magic Forest?"

A squeal from behind them caused them both to jerk around in panic.

Joe caught Ashleigh by the waistband of her jeans just as she seemed about to topple over the rail.

When he turned her around, she wrapped her arms around his neck and then leaned way back so that she could look up into his face.

"Ooh, Mr. Riley, you saved my life!" Ashleigh pressed her cheek against his as she hugged him.

Joe gulped. And wondered why Kate and Robbie were laughing.

Kate saw his confusion and relented. "Don't be taken in by her theatrics, Mr. Riley. Ash knows how to milk a scene."

"Ash wouldn'ta fallen," Robbie said, frowning at the sight of his sister clinging to the big man. "Ash never falls. She's the best athlete in our whole school."

Joe didn't care if the kid was faking it or not. The feel of the child's arms around his neck, her sweet little-girl fragrance, the fact that she'd accepted him enough to play her wiles on him, all worked to make him feel something he'd never felt before in his life. Something wonderful.

She slid out of his arms and stood on the deck looking up at him. "Can we go to Magic Forest now, Mr. Riley?" she asked sweetly.

Joe looked down at her and then at Kate. "Call me Joe, please," he said weakly.

When they left the car in the parking lot at Magic Forest, he had a twin holding each of his hands. And by the time they returned to town, they were talking about another get-together the following Sunday.

JOE LAY ON HIS MOTEL ROOM BED, his hands clasped behind his head, a dreamy smile on his face.

What a great day! A perfect day. And what great kids. Not perfect but real. He'd enjoyed their squabbling, their feistiness as much as their charm. They had a way of confronting each other that was different from regular siblings' fighting. He supposed it was a twin thing. His smile widened as he recalled some of the cute things they'd said and done during the day, pictured their faces reflecting the myriad emotions the day had wrought.

They were open to everything. No ride was too high, too fast, too frightening. No new food too exotic to try, no sight or sound too daunting. They might be awestruck but never overwhelmed.

He chuckled as he realized how fatuous his thoughts were. He was thinking like a "daddy"—a very biased daddy.

He sobered abruptly and sat up. They might not be his children at all. He was getting emotionally involved before he had the least proof they were his. He could only imagine how Matt Wilkins would react to this lack of objectivity.

Sure, the dates were right, but that was all. He was a scientist, for God's sake; he ought to know that even the dates didn't prove anything. The kids could have been a little premature—wasn't that likely with twins, anyway? If so, Monica would have had to have gotten pregnant after he left the country. Or, on the other hand, she could have been impregnated by someone else while she was seeing him. Condoms aside, accidental pregnancy still happened, and given the fact that Monica hadn't named a father on the birth certificates, it was likely she'd been at least a little promiscuous.

That thought made him wonder what kind of mother Monica would actually have been. Would the kids have been as well adjusted, as open, honest and joyous as they were if Kate hadn't been their parent? Some of it he supposed was genetic—even influenced by absent-father genes—but a lot was due to environment, to early socialization.

It occurred to him that he'd enjoyed spending the

day with Kate as much as with the children. He loved the way she interacted with the kids. That was fun. But what he especially liked was the sense of intimacy he'd felt quivering between them at odd moments. A feeling he'd never had with another woman. Something dangerous, while at the same time alluring. He hadn't felt comfortable being so evasive with her, and there'd been moments he'd felt she'd seen right through him, but there was something recklessly exciting about that, too. Especially because he knew she wasn't the person she pretended to be, either, and because she didn't know he knew.

Where to go from here? How to proceed? One thing he was sure of was that he wanted to get to know the twins better, spend as much time with them as he could. In the event that it turned out he was their father, he wanted them to like him, to trust him, when...

He pushed the thought away. He was rushing his fences again.

IT WAS ONLY LATER, as Kate was getting ready for bed, that she recalled the unanswered questions that she'd managed to bury at the back of her mind all day. Why had Joe Riley pretended to be interested in a boat charter in the first place? He said he was a journalist, but she remembered that when he'd handed out the hot dogs at Magic Forest, she'd seen that his palms were calloused. The hands of a working man, not a writer. And when she replayed their various conversations in her mind, she realized that most of his answers to her questions had been evasive.

"It takes one to know one," she jeered at herself.

Her eyes widened in shock.

Yes! Who better than someone in hiding could recognize the signs of a prevaricator?

Joe Riley was hiding his true identity. But why? Could he be a con man, maybe even a fugitive from the law? A shiver passed up her spine. Could he have been sent to find her—to find the children? He'd shown an incredible interest in the twins, bent over backward to charm them.

She began to brush her hair, her mind recalling Riley's interactions with the kids. It had seemed so natural. He'd seemed really smitten by Ashleigh and very taken with Robbie. Didn't they say children could spot a phony a mile away? And the twins had always been a little more sensitive than most.

She needed to be able to keep her objectivity. Marybeth had warned her that she was in danger of becoming emotionally handicapped by paranoia and that would reflect on the children's mental health as well.

Thank God she had Marybeth for a best friend, had been able to confide in her all those years ago when she'd first come to Lake George. At least she always had someone she could be herself with, could trust to protect her secrets while letting her vent her fears when they arose.

She could just imagine Marybeth's response when she learned that she had spent the day with the gorgeous stranger who had passed the café the other morning. Her friend would pooh-pooh all her questions, opting instead for the promise of romance in Kate's life at last.

Kate grinned at herself in the mirror. Tomorrow morning Marybeth was going to get the surprise of her life.

Chapter Four

Marybeth Simpson, owner of Kiddy Korner, pushed her glasses down on her nose and peered at the man over the rims. "You want to do what?"

Joe chuckled. This was going to be easier than he thought. "I'd like to feature your day care center in my story."

Marybeth grinned. "Why? What's so special about this place?"

"Well, the idea was to do a story about local businesses that thrive, off-season, in high-tourist areas around the state. Yours is obviously successful, and it has a human-interest slant that will appeal to readers. Almost everyone uses, or knows of a family that uses, day care, and your center has some interesting sidelines what with your latchkey program, and all." He groaned inwardly. He couldn't believe he'd said all that without stammering.

Marybeth hadn't been operating at full faculty since she looked up and saw "the hunk" standing in the hallway outside her office.

So Kate had been wrong. This wasn't just a tourist, a fly-by-night. This guy might be around for a while. He was a freelance journalist, he'd said, which meant he could work anywhere. Why, he might even like it here so much he'd decide to settle down in Lake George. She could see herself introducing him to Kate…see them gaze with immediate rapport into each other's eyes…a whirlwind romance would ensue…she'd be Kate's matron of honor…. Why, Kate would have one more layer of protection added with her married name….

"Ms. Simpson?" Joe cleared his throat and repeated her name.

Marybeth broke out of her reverie. "Hmm…well, how would you do this? I mean, would you want…like lots of long interviews?"

"I was thinking of sort of hanging out here for a few days. You have volunteer helpers sometimes, don't you? I could maybe help out while I'm getting a feel for the place."

"Free help? And free advertising? I suppose you're going to pay me as well?"

Joe was taken aback until Marybeth burst into laughter. "Just kidding, Mr. Riley." She stuck out her hand. "Call me Marybeth."

"And I'm Joe."

They shook hands.

"Come on, Joe, I'll show you around," Marybeth said.

They were halfway down the hall when Joe was attacked from behind, his name ringing out with squeals of joy.

"Joe, Joe, hey, Joe!" Robbie was wrapped around Joe's legs, preventing him from moving, while Ashleigh had leaped onto his back and was pounding him with delight.

"Joe, did you come to see us, did you, huh? You

wanta see my drawings, Joe, wanta push me on the swing? Joe, come on, I'll show you to my friends!''

Marybeth gaped at the strange, noisy tableau. When she found her voice she asked, "You know the twins?"

Joe, trying to unwind himself from the bonds of six-year-old determination, gave up and grinned helplessly at the center's director. "You could say that." He laughed and collapsed on the floor, bringing the twins down with him, laughter shaking all three of them.

It took some effort to untangle them and get the children back to their playroom, but Marybeth was determined to hear how Joe Riley, world-class hunk and presumed stranger, had become so familiar with Kate's children.

And then she was going to kill Kate for running late this morning so that she couldn't take time for breakfast and their usual morning gabfest. This was something she should have learned from Kate herself.

Joe followed Marybeth back to her office, her hand clutching his sleeve, her stride fast and purposeful.

She slammed the door of her office and turned on him.

"So, you know the Abrigado kids? How?"

Joe, still winded from the children's greeting, grinned at the woman. "This is a crime in New York State?"

Marybeth plunked her bottom against the edge of her desk and folded her arms across her chest. "Are you aware that Kate Abrigado is my best friend? That she tells me everything? That I never heard your name until you showed up here proposing your story idea?"

"We actually only met—Kate and I, I mean—on Saturday. And then we…uh, we were…I was on board the *Mermaid* for an excursion yesterday."

Was the woman on to him or was she just looking for the bare-bones gossip on her friend? He didn't care for either scenario and wasn't quite sure what this might do to blow his cover.

"That's how I met the twins. Nice kids."

Nice kids. Nothing about Kate.

"They certainly took a shine to you in a hurry," Marybeth said, peering at him over the rim of her glasses. "In fact, it looked to me like they were totally nuts about you."

Joe flushed and looked away from the woman's piercing gaze. He was here to get close to the kids, to pump her for information, to learn as much as he could about Kate before he had to reveal his purpose. He rubbed the back of his neck and returned her look.

"No accounting for taste," he said, "and especially in kids."

Marybeth could see she wasn't going to get any more out of him. She'd just have to wait and ambush Kate.

"Well," she said, pushing away from the desk, "let's hope all the children take to you so well." She gestured toward the door. "Ready to finish the tour?"

MATT WILKINS HAD LEFT his card with Don Springer, manager of the Kismet Club, with Rotterman and Hagar at HRE, and with Terri Maynard, the young woman who had been Katelynn Adams's fellow bookkeeper at HRE before the assault by the IRS.

Normally he would have considered the day wasted, since he'd certainly learned nothing from any of the interviews that would help his investigation. Strangely, he felt justified.

Springer, a short, lean man with a middle-aged

paunch that contrasted oddly with a youthful head of black hair, had been less than forthcoming, refusing to acknowledge any involvement in, or understanding of, Abrigado's murder. He had merely shrugged at the mention of Katelynn Adams's name and said, "Might have met her once." But Wilkins had sensed that the man was hiding plenty. He had a theory; if you couldn't scale a wall, you had to find a way around it. Matt intended to do just that with Springer.

Rotterman and Hagar were a true Mutt-and-Jeff combo, and even Matt, who was a tall man, had had to crane his neck to look up at the blond, light-eyed Hagar. Rotterman, closer to Matt's height, was overweight, bald and thick-lipped. Both had that same wary look and both had only repeated the same litany they'd spouted the first time he met with them; they knew nothing about Adams's whereabouts and knew nothing that could help Wilkins. Both denied ever having heard of Monica Abrigado.

Matt suspected that was a lie, because he knew the murder had been written up in the papers and carried on most of the TV newscasts. Still, he couldn't figure a connection that would account for their deceit.

Terri Maynard admitted she and Kate had been friends—"sort of"—but when Kate had just disappeared, without calling or ever getting in touch with Terri again, she had considered the friendship over. She couldn't recall that Kate had ever mentioned anything specific about her roommate, Monica Abrigado; mostly she'd talked about the fact that exchanging nighttime baby-sitting for free rent had been the best deal of her life.

"Personally," Terri had told Wilkins, "I couldn't see myself stuck with a couple of brats every night, if someone paid me a million dollars. And what was the point of saving money on rent when you were stuck home every night and had nowhere to go to spend the money?''

"Surely Kate went out sometimes, on dates or whatever," Matt had urged.

Terri had shrugged and admitted she did date now and then, but when Matt pressed for names, Terri insisted she couldn't recall that Kate had ever mentioned any.

Matt had then asked if Kate had ever talked about Abrigado's job.

"Just that she was a piano player or a singer or something like that…at a nightclub, I think.''

Did Terri Maynard know more? If she did, she wasn't forthcoming, and he'd had a feeling that if he pushed any harder he'd only alienate her.

Matt had left his card, asking Terri to call him if she remembered anything she thought might be pertinent. She'd shrugged, shown little interest, but she'd tucked his card behind the wall phone along with a haphazard bunch of notes.

He'd left and walked toward his car, feeling as if he'd just been played by an expert. Terri hadn't asked why he was investigating Adams or Abrigado, hadn't asked who he was working for and, most telling of all, hadn't shown the least surprise that someone was doing an investigation of her ex-co-worker all these years later.

He got into his car and pulled out of the spot. He rolled to the corner and was about to signal his turn when he became aware of the brown Audi three cars back. He was pretty sure he'd spotted it earlier, in the next lane on the freeway. But hell, there were probably a couple of thousand of those out there and…

He looked in his rearview mirror and saw the brown vehicle had made the turn as well. He frowned and increased his speed, taking an unplanned left at the next light. The Audi followed suit.

Matt leaned over and opened the glove compartment as he slowed and signaled a right at the next corner.

He pulled to the curb, removed the gun from the glove compartment and slid it beneath his leg, all the while keeping his eye on the mirror.

Sure enough, the Audi came around the corner. Matt was ready. Whoever it was was in for a surprise. He slipped his hand under his leg and closed it around the gun, his finger sliding onto the trigger.

The car braked, as if the driver was surprised to see Matt's car sitting there, and then sped up and drove past.

Matt tore his eyes from the mirror, turning his head to the left in order to spot the driver. But the vehicle went by in a blur of motion and Matt saw nothing but a dark shape hunched over the wheel.

He let out his breath on a long, ragged sigh and returned the gun to the glove compartment with a shaky hand. As he waited for calm to return so that he would feel safe behind the wheel, he tried to recall if the Audi had been with him all day.

"THERE'S NOTHING TO TELL," Kate insisted, brushing her hair back off her face in exasperation. "I took the kids out for an excursion and Joe…Mr. Riley…was there and we…"

"Spent the day together."

"Marybeth, you make it sound like a date. It

just…sort of happened. You're letting your romantic imagination run wild again."

"Well, you and Joe Riley can be as secretive as you want, but kids tell it like it is, and your kids have been following Joe around all day as if he was Christopher Robin and they were Pooh and Tigger."

Kate laughed at the image. "I can't believe he's actually working here."

Marybeth shook her head. "Not really working, although I admit he's been helpful to the staff. Just an extra pair of eyes and hands is a big help when we've got all the schoolkids on summer vacation as well as the usual preschoolers. But you know, I'd have expected him to be carrying a tape recorder, or making notes in a notebook all day. He must have a helluva memory."

"Maybe he's just getting a sense of the place before he begins the actual note-taking."

"So when are you going to see him again?"

"See him?" Kate strolled over to the window, pretending an interest in the empty play yard. She shrugged. "I think he mentioned something about getting together with us on the weekend. Nothing definite."

"Us? You and the kids?"

Kate turned around. "Of course. I told you, Marybeth, there's nothing romantic going on here."

A knock at the door prevented Marybeth's rebuttal.

Joe Riley stuck his head around the corner.

"Sorry to interrupt. Just wanted to say thanks, Marybeth, and I'll see you…oh! Hi, Kate."

"Mr. Riley." Kate nodded and kept her expression purposely cool, though suddenly she felt a tremor move through her body at the sight of him.

He came into the room, his grin boyish. Did he suspect his effect on her? Kate put her hands behind her, steadying herself against the windowsill.

"Did Marybeth tell you about our project? It's going to be great doing this piece, and I thought I might feature the twins in the story."

Kate's first reaction was one of pride. Her children featured in a major magazine, their adorable faces charming readers from all over the...

She gasped. "No!"

"No?" Joe frowned and Marybeth straightened in her seat, alert to Kate's sudden alarm.

Kate shook her head and tried to swallow back the panic that rose in her throat. "No, I would prefer you didn't feature the twins. In fact—" her hands curled into fists behind her back "—in fact, I don't even want them mentioned."

Joe understood her panic immediately. But he couldn't show it. "Why not? They're smart, adorable, probably photogenic as hell, and people love stuff about twins."

What excuse could she give? Kate's mind shut down as she tried to come up with a plausible argument.

Marybeth came to her rescue. "I agree with Kate, Joe. Featuring the twins would put some of the other parents' noses out of joint, and I'm sure some of the others—like Kate—will feel that they don't want their children thrust into the limelight at such an early age."

She came up and put her arm through Joe's, drawing him away from Kate, talking nonstop as she moved. "I think it would be a good idea to poll the parents and find out which ones would be interested in having their child or children featured. But all that's moot at this point, anyway, isn't it, Joe? Don't you have to focus on the center and its goals first, anyway?''

Kate breathed a sigh of thanks. The ringing in her ears drowned out the voices of the other two as she fought to control the urge to run out, grab the twins and take off for parts unknown.

She came out of her thoughts when Joe called out, ''See you, Kate,'' and the door closed behind him.

She rushed to the desk. ''Oh, thank God one of us kept a level head, Marybeth.''

Marybeth swiveled in her chair and gave her friend a sharp look. ''If he were one of the bad guys he'd have seen through that in a minute, Kate.''

Kate sank into a chair. ''I know. I just…but think about it, Marybeth. The name alone might have alerted the wrong people. And the fact that they're twins—how obvious is that?''

''I think Joe got the message, Kate. Look—'' she leaned forward and clasped Kate's hand ''—if you're still worried, I'll tell him I changed my mind about the article. There are plenty of other local businesses he can zero in on, instead.''

Kate jumped up and began pacing. ''No, I don't want that, either, Marybeth. This is a great plus for your business. We'll just have to…I'll just have to trust Joe to respect my wishes and keep the kids out of it.''

Her glance fell to the window, and she saw that Joe was leaning against his car, talking to the twins. She paused in her pacing and watched.

Joe had his hands in his pocket, his head cocked in a listening pose, as the children jabbered at him. They made a sweet picture, Kate thought, her emotions taking precedence over logic. In all these years she had never allowed herself to get involved with a man to the point where he would interact with her children. Part of that had been the built-in fear factor of living a lie, but a lot of it had to do with maternal protectiveness. She had a dread of having the children become attached to some man as a father figure and then know the heartache of losing him if things didn't work out between Kate and him. Now she wondered if she'd deprived them of a much-needed father figure, a male role model.

She looked over her shoulder at her friend. "Have the twins ever said anything to you about wishing they had a dad?"

"Not that I can recall. Of course they've always had Jon in their life, and they've spent a lot of time with the guys in your crew." Jon was Marybeth's husband, a laid-back kind of guy who had always been like an uncle to the children.

"Yeah, that's true." She turned back to the window. Ashleigh was on Joe's back, piggyback style, and Robbie was pulling him by the hand.

"I'd better rescue Mr. Riley," she said, chuckling. "The twins seem to have adopted him as their own personal jungle gym."

As she was leaving, Marybeth said quietly, "Kate, give it a rest. The past is dead. You're safe now."

When she went through the gate into the play yard, she wasn't so sure Marybeth was right. The sight of Joe standing between two swings, pushing both of the kids caused her pulse to elevate and her breath to go all thready.

He looked up and saw her, and a slow smile creased his face. "Want me to push you, too, Mom?"

Kate sank on the edge of the merry-go-round. "No,

thanks. I think I'll just sit this one out." But she couldn't help but smile in response.

"Mom, can we go to Chunky Cheese for supper? Please, please, Mom, can we?" Ashleigh wheedled.

"I hate Chunky Cheese," Robbie said, jumping off the swing and running toward Kate. "I want a hamburger. We can get toy bugs with our food."

"Yech!" Ashleigh shouted, leaping off her own swing. "Who wants bugs with their food? Why do we always have to go where he wants?"

Joe grinned at Kate, waiting to see how she'd field this one.

Kate let the kids pile on her lap and then said, quietly but firmly, "I have the money, so I get to choose."

The children started to sputter their protests, but Kate's expression remained undaunted.

"She's mean," Ashleigh said, folding her arms and pouting.

"Yeah. She's not fair," Robbie said, getting off Kate's lap and going to slump against a tree.

Ashleigh took Kate's chin in her hand and looked Kate right in the eyes. "You don't want everyone to think you're a mean mommy, do you?"

Kate stifled a laugh and tilted her head away.

"I don't care."

"You don't care?" Robbie couldn't believe his ears. "You don't care if everybody says that you're an unfair mommy, a bad, mean person?" His little body was taut with outrage and disbelief.

Kate almost choked but held firm. She shook her head. "Nope, I don't care."

Ashleigh got off Kate's lap, gave her mother one last reproachful look and shook her head. "Come on, Robbie, let's give Mommy time to think about her attitude.'' Her expression prim and disapproving, she took her brother's hand and led him off to the gate, where they huddled together discussing their mother's bad behavior in whispers.

Joe was laughing so hard he could hardly stand up. ''You're good,'' he gasped finally, wiping his eyes. ''And those kids are something else.''

Kate let the laughter out, relieved not to have to hold it in another minute. ''They can be a riot sometimes.'' She stood up.

''Guess it's time to make friends and influence six-year-olds,'' she said, smiling at Joe.

''So where will you take them?'' he asked, walking toward her.

''Home. I put their dinner in the slow cooker this morning before we left home.''

Joe nodded. ''I guess they forgot that.'' His eyes glinted as they seemed to penetrate hers.

Kate felt suddenly shy. ''Apparently.'' She knew she should move, join the kids and go home. She brushed her hand down the side of her black-watch plaid skirt, rebuttoned the matching jacket.

''Listen, I was thinking…'' Joe lowered his gaze and dug a line in the dirt with the toe of his shoe. ''Uh, how about having dinner with me one night this week?''

''Dinner?''

''Yeah…um…just the two of us.'' He cleared his throat. ''A grown-up thing.''

''Without the kids?''

''Well, yeah. I thought maybe the Cove. Doesn't seem like the kind of place kids would enjoy, anyway.''

''Look, Mr. Riley…Joe. I'm really not into dating

much right now. We're getting into the season and the kids are out of school, and…''

"And you don't have any kind of social life."

"I beg your pardon?"

He shrugged and dug his hands deeper into his pockets. Kate looked away from what that did to the front of his khakis.

"You don't seem to do much more than work and spend time with your kids."

"How would you know?"

Could Joe Riley be the guy she'd felt was following her all week? But why? If he was connected in any way to the people who had murdered Monica, he'd had plenty of chances to do her and the kids harm. Why hang around, pretend to be doing an article?

"I don't. But I don't see anybody else hanging around waiting to ask you to dinner."

Kate's instinct was to refuse. She still had a feeling of uneasiness with this man, a sense that he wasn't exactly what he presented himself to be. On the other hand, her best friend liked him and would urge her to accept. Yeah, but Marybeth was a hard-core romantic seriously out of touch with reality when the alternative was fantasy.

Maybe going out with the guy would give her a chance to dig a little, loosen him up so she could subtly ply him with questions.

"What night?"

"Well…Wednesday night."

"All right." She was almost ashamed of how ungracious that sounded.

Joe's smile almost made her change her mind. *Beware of handsome men, they may be hazardous to your health.*

"I'll pick you up at seven, if that's all right."

"Seven. Sure." She glanced over at the children, who were regarding the two of them with solemn, waiting faces.

"I'd better go."

"Right. See you Wednesday."

Joe waved at the kids and took off with a long, confident stride.

Kate joined the children, her emotions fluctuating between dread and excitement.

Chapter Five

Marybeth stood at the edge of the playground and watched as Joe Riley took turns pushing the twins on the swings. To be fair, he also pushed the other two children who were swinging, but throughout the day she'd observed that Joe was never far from the Abrigado children. She'd seen parents who spent less time with their own offspring when they spent a volunteer day at the center. What was Joe's big attraction to the twins?

A smile softened her face as awareness dawned. Of course! Kate. The guy was playing up to the kids to impress their mother. Kate had told her this morning at breakfast that she had a dinner date with Joe tomorrow night. She'd tried to pass it off as no big deal, but Marybeth knew Kate better than anyone, and she knew Kate was plenty excited about the date.

She was about to go back into the building when she heard Robbie's voice raised in anger.

"Joe's our special friend. He belongs to us."

"Yeah," Ashleigh echoed, "he's our Joe."

"Well, you're supposed to share," Billy Cameron shouted back.

"Don't have to," Robbie insisted.

Marybeth was about to intervene when Joe recovered from his obvious dismay and stepped in.

"Hey, kids, listen. I'm here to help Marybeth and the other staff." He'd squatted so that he was at eye level with the kids and had a hand on each of the two little boys' arms, keeping them separated. For once, Ashleigh appeared to be listening rather than rushing headlong into battle.

"When I'm here at the center, it's so I can be with all the kids." He looked at Robbie. "That doesn't mean we aren't still special friends, Rob, it just means that we have to be fair about this."

Ashleigh moved over and put her hand on Joe's shoulder, patting it maternally. "It's okay, Joe. We know you like us bestest."

"Does not!" Billy screamed.

This time Marybeth stepped into the fray. It took her exactly two minutes to get the three children separated and sent off to different projects, and then she ordered Joe to her office in almost exactly the same I-will-tolerate-no-nonsense tone of voice.

She went to her desk and ordered Joe to sit down.

He did so. Meekly.

"Joe, this isn't the first time I've observed the twins' special attachment to you. I think, on principle, that it's great that the three of you hit it off, but when it starts causing chaos here, it has to be nipped in the bud."

Joe nodded, a look of chagrin on his face. "I didn't mean to start trouble. The kids met me before I came to the center, so I guess they feel sort of proprietorial. I'll try to be more—"

"I think it's more than that, Joe," Marybeth interrupted. "I'm wondering if there isn't some danger inherent in this situation."

"Danger? Come on, Marybeth, what do you think, I'm some kind of child molester?" He was on his feet, outrage etched in every muscle of his body.

For a moment, Marybeth stared at him, her mouth agape. His stance was exactly like Ashleigh's when she went on one of her tirades. What was this, adults using kids as role models?

"I wasn't thinking anything of the kind, Joe. You're not even in the ballpark with that one."

"So what's so dangerous?"

Marybeth picked up one of the jacks on her desktop and spun it on one of its spikes. God, she hated to admit she'd been wrong. But she'd been thinking only of Kate's nonexistent sex life, not the children. Maybe she could do something to remedy that.

"Joe, you're just passing through. You do a story, you move on. You get involved with people—women—along the way, no big deal. They're adults, they know the score. But kids, well, that's a different matter. Kids like the twins, without dads of their own, they get attached to some guy, and when he moves on, they're left holding emotional baggage. It's like sending them the message, over and over, don't trust any man, don't love any man, 'cause they're not here for the duration."

Joe stared at the woman, his mouth still clamped in residual anger, his mind spinning. Marybeth was right on target. Just exactly how much was he actually thinking about the children's welfare? What were his intentions, after all? Suppose the twins turned out to be his. Did he mean to grab them and run? To where? He was due back at his job in less than six weeks. What then? As long as he was assigned stateside, he'd most likely work out of New York. But what if he got sent overseas again? Kids needed stability. Could a man, a bachelor, offer them that?

And then his mind flipped the coin. What if the children weren't his, after all? What if all his efforts to find the truth only brought disaster to this happy little family, leaving the children without a mother or father?

Because the bottom line was there was no way to determine his paternity without exposing Kate.

He needed to rethink where he was going with this. Maybe pass it by Matt. The older man had a way of cutting through the bull and getting to the truth of the matter.

"I guess I've got enough now to cut back on my time here," he told Marybeth, suddenly feeling ashamed at the subterfuge he'd been playing.

He guessed he wasn't cut out to be a detective after all, didn't have the stomach for the deceptions and wasn't even all that good at it.

"We'll miss having you around, Joe," Marybeth admitted, knowing it was probably best for the twins if Joe curtailed his involvement with them.

Maybe it was time to turn over what he knew to a lawyer, someone who knew how this should be handled. Someone who could be objective.

He'd pass that by Matt, too.

MATT WILKINS STOOD in the doorway of his office, a chill chasing up and down his spine. Someone had been here.

Not a fastidious man, certainly not obsessive, Matt nevertheless had a definite sense of order. He didn't, for instance, leave his file cabinet drawers open after he'd filed or removed a case folder. He didn't push his desk chair three feet from his desk and just leave it there. He didn't leave the lights on when he left at night.

He rushed to the file cabinet and searched through the files in the drawer that was standing open. The one he was looking for was missing. He fumbled through the stack again, thinking it might be misfiled. It wasn't there.

He pushed his chair back in place and grabbed the phone. His fingers fumbled as he punched in numbers and misdialed. He had to hang up and redial, and then he grabbed the phone and began pacing with it in his hand as he waited for the clerk at the Lake George Inn to connect him with Riley's room.

Joe answered on the third ring. When he recognized Matt's voice, he started to tell him that he was having some doubts.

Impatiently, Matt interrupted him. "Joe, listen to me. We've got a problem. Someone broke into my office, and I'm afraid they may know where Katelynn Adams is."

For a moment Joe said nothing, and then he began to sputter questions.

"Joe, Joe! I'll fill you in on the details later. Right now I think you need to get to Adams. Warn her. I think I've been followed, and if I have, that means that Adams…"

He spun around as he heard a noise behind him. He stared at the man standing in the doorway holding a gun.

"What the hell…" he cried out.

The man shot him.

Matt fell to the floor, taking the phone with him.

The man strode across the room, knelt beside the body and felt for a pulse. Finding none, he nodded in satisfaction, withdrew the phone from the lifeless hand and lifted the receiver to his ear.

"Matt...what's going on, Matt! Matt! Are you there? Was that a gunshot...Matt!"

The man returned the handset to the base and placed it on the desk.

He was about to leave when a thought occurred to him.

He lifted the receiver of the phone and pressed the redial button.

"Lake George Inn," a cheerful voice announced. "How may I help you?"

The man hung up the phone, a smug smile on his face, stepped over Wilkins's body and left the office.

JOE FRANTICALLY FUMBLED in his wallet, looking for Matt's number, his mind refusing to provide the number from memory.

The phone in Matt's office rang ten times before the answering machine kicked in. Joe pressed the cutoff button without saying a word, his hands shaking as he hung up.

Was it a gunshot he heard? His mind rejected the thought; it was unacceptable. A car backfiring. That had to be it. Matt had to have been calling him from his car phone, probably while at a standstill in rush-hour traffic, and a car near his had backfired.

But Joe's hands wouldn't stop shaking, and a sense of dread invaded him. An image of Matt falling kept pushing at his mind. The panic in Matt's voice had been real, a sense of urgency that had quivered over the wires.

He sat on the edge of the bed, his hand still resting on the phone, and tried to make sense of what Matt

had said, what he'd implied. Somebody knew about
Kate, might know where she was. But what somebody?
And did that mean Kate was in danger? And if Kate
was in danger, so were the twins!

First he dialed 911 to have someone check on Matt.
Then he shot to his feet. He had to get to Kate. Warn
her.

KATE OPENED HER FRONT DOOR and did a double take
when she saw Joe Riley standing on her porch.

"Wow," she said with a laugh, "you must be really
anxious. You're a day early for our dinner date. Or are
you just incredibly hungry?"

Joe moved past her in a rush, calling over his shoulder. "Close the door, quick!"

Automatically Kate obeyed. But as soon as it closed
she spun around, a sense of dread swamping her.

"What's going on, Joe? What are you doing here?
Why are you—"

"No time, Kate, we've got to get out of here!" He
ran to the staircase and looked up, one foot already on
the first riser as if he meant to charge the stairs.
"Where are the kids?"

"In…in their rooms. Joe, what are you yelling
about? What do you mean I have to get out of here?"

She backed away from him, suddenly afraid of the
man who looked nearly demented, his breath coming
in quick pants, his face flushed and damp with perspiration. The twins. Did he mean to harm her children?

She rushed forward, planning to push him away from
the staircase, to put herself between him and the children.

"I think you'd better leave, Joe, this isn't—"

He grabbed her arms, forcing her to face him. "Kate,

you're not listening. You have to get the kids and come with me. We have to get out of here. Now!''

Outrage swamped her, made her dizzy. ''Are you crazy? We're not going anywhere with you. You must be mad to think—''

Joe forced himself to at least appear calm. ''Kate, I think you're in danger. I think someone's coming after you and I want you to—''

''Who are you?'' Kate's voice rang out, sounding a lot stronger than she was feeling at the moment. It was like déjà vu…Monica's voice on the phone quivering with fear and urgency…escaping into the night with the babies…the car pulling up to the brownstone only seconds after she'd pulled away from the curb….

''I'll explain later. Right now, you have to pack enough stuff for a couple of days for you and the twins and get out of here.''

It was worse than déjà vu. It was happening for real, all over again. Anger surfaced, overcoming fear.

''I don't know who the hell you are. For all I know you could be the real threat. I'm tired of being ordered to pack up two kids and take off in the night with no knowledge of what I'm running from, where I'm going to.'' Her chin thrust out in belligerence. ''This time I'm not budging until I get some information.'' She clamped her hands on the stair banister and glared at Joe.

Joe pushed her aside and ran up the stairs. ''Move your butt, Adams. I'll tell you everything when we're on the road, when I've got you somewhere safe. I figure we've got about five hours tops before they get here, and if you won't get the kids ready, I will.''

Adams. He'd called her by her real name. For a moment she was too stunned to move. And then reason moved her to action.

She was on his heels when he charged into Robbie's room, calling out for Ashleigh, trying to keep hysteria out of her voice as she announced that they were all going on a little vacation.

It was almost impossible to pack with her hands shaking so badly. She could hear the children's excited voices intermingling with the low rumbling of Joe's. She hesitated in front of her closet, her mind momentarily refusing to function. Holding the bag open, she snatched and shoved clothing into it, not thinking at all. She turned on her heels and stared at her dresser. Underwear, she thought, rushing back to raid the top drawer. She scooped the few things on top of the chest of drawers in on top of the lingerie, not bothering to discriminate. She tore the drawer out of the bedside table, leaving it on the floor where it fell and stooped to retrieve her personal telephone book.

Work. Somewhere along the way they'd have to stop so she could make some phone calls, arrange for Valerie, her assistant, to take over in her absence, leave orders for Valerie and Captains Drake and Martin, let Marybeth know…

She was about to leave the room, but something nagged at her, making her feel she was forgetting something important. Her gaze fell on the dresser and the small, framed photo of her parents. Of course! She couldn't leave her only memento of her mother and father behind. She slipped it into her backpack and put her mind back in gear as she left the room.

"Let's go, Kate!"

Joe. Panic froze her blood, numbed her limbs, setting

up a roar of white noise in her head. She couldn't do this, couldn't…couldn't…

Joe grabbed the duffel, slung it over his shoulder and slung an arm around her waist.

"It's okay, Kate. It's going to be fine." He moved her toward the door, whispering soothing sounds in her ear as he maneuvered her toward the stairs. Vaguely she was aware of the children's voices, the sound of a car door slamming, the phone ringing.

She seemed to be moving through fog, her vision blurred, her sense of space horribly altered so that her feet couldn't quite anticipate the next step.

Vaguely she became aware that she was sitting in the front seat of Joe's car, that somehow the seat belt was fastened around her, that the car was moving. She bent her head, tried to focus on her breathing, tried to push back the waves of nausea that threatened.

A firm, large hand was on her back, moving in a circular motion. She felt the heat of it begin to penetrate the cold, felt the dizziness begin to abate.

"Mommy, where are we going?" Ashleigh. Her voice shrill with excitement. Kate lifted her head, rubbed her hands over her face, swallowed the tears that threatened.

"We're…we're…" Her voice was a croak. She cleared her throat and glanced helplessly at Joe, noting the grim set of his face in profile.

"We're going wherever we want," Joe said, his cheerful tone belying the set of his jaw. His hand snaked out and grasped hers, squeezing, warning.

"That's not a vacation," Robbie scoffed. "A vacation is when you're going someplace on purpose and when you get there you sign your name in a book and they give you a room with two beds and a really cool bathroom and you get tickets for free rides.''

Joe chuckled. The sound surprised Kate with its tone of normalcy. She fumbled in her bag, found a tissue, blew her nose. Another normal sound.

"Is not," Ashleigh refuted. "A vacation is when you don't have to go to school and Mommy doesn't have to go to work and you don't have to set the alarm clock. Right, Joe?"

"Sounds like you're both experts on vacations," Joe said, sending a reassuring grin at Kate.

The children began touting all the vacations they'd had, expanding on each other's memories. Kate found herself drawn into the discussion as they punctuated every statement with the words "'Member, Mommy?"

She felt herself becoming grounded, the invasion of panic steadily receding.

Gradually the blur of scenery outside her window became familiar, well-known landmarks alerting her to their progress. They were driving south; peripherally she glimpsed a green sign decreeing Connecticut ahead.

"Mommy! You forgot to give us supper," Ashleigh accused.

"I'm star-ar-ving," Robbie moaned, making it sound as though he hadn't eaten in a week.

"McDonald's?" Joe asked in a murmur.

"McDonald's rocks!" Robbie yelled.

"No, it doesn't," Ashleigh argued. "I like Burger King. Burger King is the bomb!"

"Rocks? Bombs?" Joe looked askance at Kate.

Kate shrugged. "It means they like something." What kind of man didn't know the current slang that children, and plenty of adults, used to express pleasure?

She needed to get out of this car, out of earshot of the children, needed to shout at Joe, to demand answers.

Joe took the off-ramp at the next exit and turned toward the familiar arch. As he followed the entrance arrows to the drive-through he spotted the playground. He spun the wheel, lurching out of the drive-through lane, and eased into a parking place outside the restaurant.

"How about we eat inside and then you kids can play on the playground for a bit while your mom and I have our coffee." He laughed at the twins' exaggerated cries of delight.

It took an interminable time, it seemed to Kate, to get everyone's order taken, to get situated at a table, to get through the business of eating. She was surprised when she looked down and saw that all of her fish sandwich and most of her French fries were gone. She couldn't recall chewing, swallowing. The hollow feeling in her stomach was unrelieved by the lump of food that sat there, threatening to eject at any moment.

At last the children were through, sauce wiped from Robbie's chin, Ashleigh's sweater buttoned properly, Joe balancing two covered cups of coffee in one hand while the other held the door for Kate. She called out to the children to watch both ways when crossing the parking lot, waiting to make sure they obeyed. When she saw them safely through the gate into the play area she took a deep breath and followed Joe to the car.

"Hold these," Joe said, handing her the cups. He started up the car and drove to the other side of the lot so that they faced the playground. The twins were already at the top of the chute slide.

He shut off the engine, turned sideways, took one of the cups from her and heaved a deep sigh.

Kate stared at him, her mind buzzing with questions, her throat unable to release one of them.

"Where to begin?" Joe began.

Kate waited. She wanted to scream, to pummel him with her fists. She wanted to cry. She did none of those. She waited.

Joe nodded, reading her mind, and sighed again. "Okay, here goes. I knew Monica, dated her. I'm a petroleum geologist. The company I work for sent me to Saudi Arabia. I lost touch with Monica. The assignment went on for longer than I'd anticipated. I just arrived back in the country a couple of weeks ago."

He stopped, took a sip of his coffee. He turned and looked out of the windshield, watched the children for a moment. "I decided to look up some of my old friends. Monica no longer had a phone listing, so when I happened to be in the neighborhood, I stopped by the building she'd lived in when I knew her, thinking someone might know where she'd moved."

He went on to tell her about his conversation with the super, about his meeting with Detective Vatterott. He didn't tell her about going to city hall, looking up the birth records.

Kate listened. She said nothing until he told her about hiring Matt Wilkins.

She suddenly became aware of the sun blazing through the windshield, intensifying the heat in the car. She rolled her window down, gulping thirstily at the fresh air.

"Why?"

"Why what?"

"Why did you hire a private detective? Why is it

important for you to continue an investigation the police have obviously deemed unnecessary?''

Joe swallowed more coffee, barely registering that it was now lukewarm. He needed to wet his throat against the sudden dryness. How much to tell her? Would she trust him if she knew he intended to question the paternity of the children? Would she become more frightened, more defensive, less apt to reveal any of her own story?

A car pulled into the lot and he found himself watching in the rearview mirror as two men got out and went into the building.

This wasn't the time to alarm her. He had to protect her, and in order to do that, he needed her cooperation, her trust.

''I had learned about you and the twins, about your disappearance. I felt I owed it to Monica to try to find you, to make sure her children were well-cared-for.''

Kate studied him, looking for signs of dissembling. His eyes crinkled at the corners, as if they'd become used to squinting against sunlight. He said he'd been in Saudi Arabia. It would explain the intensity of his tan. She noticed the glints of gold in his hair, a natural bleaching from the sun. God, he was so handsome. Even with the window open at her side, she became aware of the confined space they shared.

Concentrate, Kate, she told herself, this is no time for sexual chemistry.

''Owed it to her? I don't understand.''

He looked up, meeting her eyes. She hadn't touched her coffee. It sat on the dashboard, unopened. She was sitting against the door, her arms clasped around her waist as if she were cold, but he could see tiny beads of perspiration on her skin. There was something so fragile about her, though he knew she was a strong, resourceful woman. Tough.

There was nothing tough about her looks, though. Wisps of hair that had escaped her braid were a shimmering halo of fire around her face, emphasizing her creamy complexion, the intense green of her eyes. Joe's breath became shallow as he inhaled her fragrance, wafting toward him on the breeze that blew past her through the open window.

He reached up to loosen his tie. A futile gesture. He wasn't wearing a tie. He sensed his own vulnerability and shook his head.

"I'm not sure. We were close…good friends…"

Kate's felt a click go off in her head. "Lovers," she said.

Joe hesitated. "Well…yes. Briefly."

For a moment Kate felt something akin to loss. As if someone had hurt her feelings or betrayed her. She didn't understand the feeling and pushed it away, letting anger replace it.

"And that gave you the right to hire someone to look for me, to disrupt my life, to put me in danger? Not to mention my children?"

His self-defense mechanism was anger that matched hers. "Not *your* children, Ms. Adams! Monica Abrigado's children."

She was prepared to argue, had already taken the deep breath necessary to raise her voice, to scream objections at him, when the children came running up to the car.

"Joe, we're done playing. We want to go on vacation now, Joe."

Joe flinched, aware that he'd said too much, that he'd

alienated her in the worst possible way and at a time when he most needed her to trust him.

It was with both relief and regret that he leaned over, opened the back door and told the twins that they were indeed going on vacation now.

With his lack of experience with children, he hadn't anticipated the way kids could defuse an emotionally charged atmosphere. Before they'd driven another twenty-five miles, they were all playing travel games and Kate was laughing and caught up in the spirit of "vacation" and Joe found himself joining in with pleasure.

It was already dark and after nine when they crossed the border into Connecticut. The children's high spirits were beginning to flag.

"I think we should stop at a motel for the night and get an early start in the morning," Joe said softly.

Kate, who was fiddling with the radio dial, glanced over and nodded. "Yes. The kids need a break."

There was a coffee shop adjacent to the motel they chose, and after they'd registered for adjoining rooms, Kate's with a second bed for the children, Joe went over to get an order of sandwiches and milk while Kate bathed the twins.

"Can we watch TV, Mommy?" Robbie begged as Kate unwrapped their sandwiches and stuck straws in their milk cartons.

Kate was about to suggest it was too late when Ashleigh joined her brother's plea.

"We can eat in the other room," Joe suggested.

"All right, you two, but just until you finish your food," Kate warned as she picked up her own sandwich.

Joe stifled a chuckle as he saw that the children's

chewing suddenly went into slow motion. At that rate, they'd be a good hour eating their meal.

Kate rolled her eyes and shook her head. "You've got twenty minutes, and then it's bedtime whether you've finished eating or not."

They left the room to the sounds of the twins' giggles.

"I'm sorry about what I said earlier," Joe began, pulling out a chair at the table in his room.

Kate sat down and looked up at him. "We were both stressed." She looked down at her hands in her lap as Joe took a seat across from her.

"Do you have any idea who would want to hurt me...or the children?" When she raised her eyes, they were liquid with vulnerability.

"Not yet. But it would help if you'd tell me exactly what happened the night you took off with the babies."

Their sandwiches forgotten, Joe settled back to listen as Kate told her story.

Chapter Six

Joe listened with grave attention as Kate described the details of the night she'd left the city with another woman's babies, in fear for her life and theirs, and as she itemized each step she'd taken to delete the past and prepare for the future. The only thing Kate left out was the business about the key. She hadn't taken it, anyway, and for some reason she felt it was wiser to make no mention of it.

Joe was overwhelmed by the woman's resourcefulness, intelligence and courage. But not so overwhelmed that her story raised no questions in his mind.

"Why didn't you drive right to the nearest police precinct?" was his first question.

"You had to be there, to hear the panic in Monica's voice—and at some level I was afraid that what she was involved with was illegal. I acted on instinct. Ran!"

"And what about after? When you knew she was dead. Wasn't that the time to go to the cops?"

"That was when I knew the danger she'd feared was real. Whoever killed her might still come after us, and I didn't dare risk the children's safety by coming forward. There was nothing I could tell the police. I knew nothing about Monica's business or her death. And then, a few days later, they announced they'd found her killer, so..."

"What about the father?"

Kate looked confused. "What father?"

"The twins' father," Joe snapped. "Why didn't you contact him?"

Kate's jaw dropped and her eyes met Joe's honestly. "I never knew who fathered the twins. For that matter, I don't think Monica did. From what little she said, I got the idea she'd been...careless...in her relationships, I mean."

"And you didn't try to find out, after her death?"

Kate winced at the accusatory note.

"When...how would I have done that? When the birth certificates arrived, I saw that the father was listed as unknown...what could I have done? The kids needed a roof over their heads. That was my first priority, and for all I knew, it might have been the twins' father who had been the person Monica feared."

Joe shrugged, irritated as much with himself as with her. This was territory he really wasn't ready to explore.

"So you pretended they were yours and—"

Kate interrupted, her eyes flashing. "They were mine! They were just babies, nine months old. They didn't even remember Monica after a few days. They knew me as well as they knew her. After I lost my job, I'd spent almost more time with them than she had. And then—" she hesitated, a pink flush coloring her skin "—when they began to talk, they called me 'Mommy.' What was I supposed to tell a couple of toddlers? They needed a mother and I was all they had.

It wasn't as if Monica was ever coming back to reclaim them!''

Joe realized they'd reached an impasse. He wasn't yet ready to show his hand, and he had a feeling Kate was still holding something back. But for the moment, they needed a united front if they were to keep ahead of whoever was after Kate and the kids. They needed to pull together.

''I'd better get the kids in bed,'' Kate said, rising from her place at the table.

''You didn't eat,'' Joe said, gesturing toward her untouched food.

''I'm not very hungry, after all. I think I'll get the kids down and then take a shower.''

Joe watched her through the open connecting door as she readied the children for bed. He listened as she read them a bedtime story, fielded their questions and then bent to tuck them in with kisses.

Her mothering of them was so natural, as if they were really her own flesh and blood. He guessed that nurturing came easily to some women and she was one of them. It made him think about all her aspects; she was a good business woman, a soft, nurturing mother, a devoted, loyal friend, and she had shown incredible serenity and foresightedness under stress. That made her kind of unique. A woman who would grace a man's life. For some reason, he thought of Matt Wilkins. Matt would like Kate. It made him realize he'd begun to think of Matt as more than a professional contact— Matt was his first friend since he'd returned home.

And Matt would see through any of her guises if she wasn't all she seemed.

He went over to the phone. He'd try Matt's number

again. If he didn't reach him, he'd try again in the morning.

Matt wasn't there. Joe hung up silently, praying that what he'd heard hadn't been a gunshot. He reached for the TV remote control. Anything to chase the doubts and fears away. What if it had been a gunshot and Matt was hurt? First thing in the morning, if he still couldn't reach the detective, he'd try all the hospitals in Manhattan.

He was just in time to catch the news.

Kate was just about to go into the shower when she heard a cry from the other room. She dropped the robe and gown she'd just taken from her bag and rushed to the door.

Joe was on his knees in front of the TV set, his hands over his mouth, his eyes wide and staring.

"Wilkins's body was discovered by the night cleaning crew. At this time, the police have no leads."

Kate gasped and took a step into the room. Tears were running down Joe's face and he was rocking back and forth.

"I knew it...I knew it...I killed him...." A sob tore from his throat.

Kate rushed to his side, kneeling next to him, and put her arms around his shaking body. "No, Joe! This isn't your fault. How could it be? You were in Lake George, you didn't..."

"You don't understand!" Joe gasped. He swiped at his wet face with his fists. "Matt was working for me. It was the only case he was handling. When I hired him I signed his death warrant!"

Kate fell back on her heels. "Joe—aren't you making too much of this?"

Joe stared at her, glaring. "A man is dead. A man who was my friend. I'm making too much of this?"

"Joe, you're going too far with this mea culpa business. You don't even know for sure that Wilkins was killed by someone connected to your case. He had cases before—maybe he stepped on someone's toes, went too far in an investigation. Maybe he was the cause of someone's divorce or someone ending up in jail and…"

Her voice fell away as Joe got to his feet and brushed past her. He sat on the edge of the bed and reached for the phone.

"Who are you calling?"

"That cop I talked to at the Fourteenth—maybe he knows something that wasn't on the news. He was the guy who referred me to Matt Wilkins in the first place."

"Good idea." He was already dialing. "I guess I'll go take my shower, then."

She stood under the spray a long time, letting the hot water ease the stiffness of the hours in the car, the tensions of the nightmare that seemed never-ending.

She thought about Joe in tears. She'd never seen a man cry before. It was a powerful sight. And she knew Joe had only known Matt Wilkins a brief time. Either Joe Riley was an extremely sensitive, caring man or…

She couldn't envision an alternative.

She thought about the first time she'd been forced to run. She'd been totally in control; every move she made was of her own volition, every choice her own. And she'd made a plan and followed through. Did Joe have a plan? It didn't look like it to her. And now this new horror, the private detective killed.

The correlation between that time and this suddenly

struck her. The danger, the run, hearing the news on a TV newscast in a motel room...

More déjà vu. More coincidences.

Uneasiness weakened her limbs, numbed her mind. She slumped against the shower stall wall and folded her arms around herself.

Did it matter, help in any way, that there were two of them now? *Two heads better than one, two for the price of one, two for the seesaw...too many cooks spoil the broth...*

She giggled and wiped the tears and water from her face. "I'm losing it," she whispered. "I'm cracking up." She turned off the water and reached for a towel.

She'd pulled herself together by the time she put the hair dryer down and tied the belt of her robe.

The children were sleeping peacefully, ignorant of lurking dangers, innocent of subterfuge and malice. She tiptoed past them and went to the connecting door, still slightly ajar.

Joe was sitting on the bed, propped up with pillows against the headboard. The only light in the room was the bluish cast from the TV screen.

"Joe," she said softly, "did you talk to the guy?"

Joe shook his head. "Nothing. They don't have a clue."

"Well, it's early yet." She started to turn, and her gaze fell on the TV screen. On it was one of her all-time favorite movies. She lingered in the doorway, watching as the wedding scene unfolded.

"Ever see this movie?" Joe asked from the bed.

Kate nodded. "Mmm-hmm, one of my favorites."

They watched a moment in silence.

"Why don't you come in and watch it?" Joe said.

Kate considered. Maybe just this part. The table was

a few feet away. She pulled out a chair and sat down, folding her hands together on the tabletop, her back straight, her bare feet tucked under her gown.

After a few minutes she altered her position, trying to get more comfortable.

"Why don't you sit over here," Joe suggested. "Much more comfortable."

She glanced over and shook her head. "No, thanks. I'm fine." But she wasn't, she realized a short time later. Her back was beginning to ache and she was tired of sitting.

She glanced over at Joe.

He caught the look and gestured her over. "Come on," he said, "there's plenty of room."

There was. Kate got up and went to the bed. Joe relinquished one of his pillows, setting it against the headboard with plenty of room between them. Kate settled back, sighing with relief at the comfort.

They watched in silence for a few minutes, and then Joe asked in a near whisper, "What was your life like before? You know, before that night?"

Kate kept her eyes on the screen, but she considered his question. Her life before that night, before she'd become a full-time mother. Dating, dreaming improbable fantasies, ultimately being responsible for no one but herself.

"I worked for Hudson River Excursions, another excursion boat company in Yonkers. They ran paddleboats on the Hudson. I did bookkeeping and helped out with setting up excursions and charters."

"Did you like the job?"

"Yes. Very much. I loved working near the river and all the different aspects of the riverboat business."

"But you left."

"Yes. But I didn't quit."

She turned sideways, facing him, drawing her knees up, her arm bent under her head. "Actually, the strangest thing happened. The IRS or some agency like that shut them down. It happened without warning. We were all over at the bar and grill across the street having lunch. When we went back to work, there were yellow tapes around the building and agents everywhere. They let us go in to get our personal belongings and then we were escorted out."

"Then what did you do?"

Kate smiled, remembering. "Monica treated the whole thing like it was no big deal. I was already babysitting at night in exchange for rent. She insisted that it was worth the extra hours' sleep in the morning to cover my share of the utilities and groceries if I'd take care of the babies in the mornings as well. Sort of become their nanny."

"So you didn't bother looking for another job?"

Kate ran her finger over the nubby surface of the chenille bedspread. "I planned to. I was free in the afternoons to go job-hunting. But it was only a week later that Monica called and…"

Her eyelashes were dark and thick against her cheeks, and her skin was almost translucent in the light from the TV. Joe had noticed the fresh, soapy scent of her skin and freshly shampooed hair when she joined him on the bed. Despite the fact that she wore both a gown and robe, Joe found himself thinking about the fact that she wore nothing underneath.

Maybe it hadn't been such a good idea to invite her into the room, onto the bed.

He made a point of returning his attention to the movie.

Kate felt suddenly shy. He'd turned from her so abruptly. Had she been boring him? She thought about getting up and leaving and then thought if she did that, he'd think he'd hurt her feelings. She certainly didn't want to have him think she cared that much.

She turned back, stretched out her legs and refocused on the film.

The scene with the bride's father shooting at birds made them both laugh, softly, so they wouldn't disturb the sleeping children. They exchanged a glance of mutual appreciation.

"Did you ever go over that phone conversation in your mind, try to recall anything Monica might have said that would have indicated what she was so afraid of?"

It took a moment for Kate to make the transition from the scene on the screen to Joe's question.

"Only about a zillion times," she said, keeping her eyes on the movie. She waited a moment and then glanced over at him, shaking her head. "There was nothing. It was all very abstract. And very traumatic." Her gaze returned to the TV set. "Oh, I love this part."

They watched, laughing again and then sobering at a dramatic moment in the movie.

"Were you in love with Monica?"

Joe jerked his head around, but Kate stared straight ahead, stunned by the question she'd blurted aloud.

"In love...?" He didn't think he'd ever even thought the word. Certainly he'd never said it aloud. "No. We dated a little and then we, uh..."

Kate nodded, still staring at the screen, "Made love."

"Had sex."

She couldn't look at him, couldn't let him see the

relief that flooded her, yet she didn't understand the feeling. Joe Riley's love life, past or present, was no business of hers.

"We both knew nothing was going to come of it," Joe continued. "I knew I was going overseas and her singing career was her priority. We were more friends than anything else. We both knew it wasn't going any further than that."

"Very nineties," Kate murmured.

"Very realistic," Joe amended.

Very cold and unemotional, Kate thought. She thought about Monica, who had always been so bubbly, so warm. She'd never seen Monica with any man, although she knew her friend had a relationship with Don Springer, the owner of the Kismet. Kate had always assumed Monica wanted to keep her love life and her home life separate because of the babies.

Joe stared straight ahead, glad of the semidarkness of the room, uncomfortably aware that his feelings towards Kate Adams were becoming much warmer than was good for either of them.

They watched the movie, which had come to a sad scene.

Next to him, Kate sniffled. Joe glanced over and saw the shiny streaks on her face. He got up, went into the bathroom and returned with a box of tissues. He got back on the bed and handed her a couple.

Kate blotted her eyes, blew her nose and smiled gratefully. Joe grinned and looked back toward the TV. Beside him, Kate snuggled down a little more on the pillow.

A few minutes later Kate heard a kind of choking sound and turned her head to see that Joe was very moved by the scene they were watching. She leaned over and rubbed his arm.

"You okay?" she whispered.

He nodded, blew his nose and grinned sheepishly. "Rough scene," he whispered back hoarsely.

They lay side by side, only their faces turned toward each other's, their expressions sober.

"Have you ever had anyone really sick like that?" Kate asked, referring to the hospital scene on the screen.

Joe nodded. "My mom died when I was twelve. Cancer. It was pretty bad."

Kate rubbed his arm again but said nothing.

"You?"

Kate shook her head. "My parents were killed in a car accident on their way home from my graduation from college." It was still difficult to say the words, even after all this time. She was grateful when Joe didn't make a banal comment of sympathy but changed the subject, instead.

"Where was home?"

"Seattle."

He grinned. "The other side of the country. When you leave home, you *really* leave home."

She smiled back at him. "No sense doing things halfway."

"You're kind of an expert at running away."

Was that a criticism? Kate frowned. "I'm an expert at protecting myself," she rebutted. But there wasn't much anger in her tone. The room was warm, the bed comfortable. Suddenly she felt a languid weariness creeping over her. She stifled a yawn and glanced over at the TV. The four main characters were in the cemetery. She tried to watch and found her vision blurring. She shut her eyes.

Joe tried to focus on the movie, but fatigue seemed to have crept over him and he couldn't keep his eyes open. He turned and his head touched Kate's. He knew he should pull back, move away. He meant to. He wondered why she didn't pull away; and then his mind shut down.

White noise from the TV awakened Kate. She opened her eyes and found herself staring into the sleeping face of Joe Riley. Oh, God, she'd fallen asleep beside him. In bed with him.

She tried to sit up and discovered that his arm was pinning her down. How had that happened? Surely they hadn't...? She breathed relief when she recalled the moment she'd drifted off.

Lord, he was even more handsome up close like this. The light from the TV set allowed her to see clearly the strong planes of his face, the stubble of beard growth, the fine shape of his eyebrows. Her gaze traveled to the V-neck of his T-shirt where a soft mat of hair grazed the opening, and then to the sleekly muscled arm below the short sleeve. She could smell his breath puffing softly from his slightly open mouth— sweet, clean and warm on her skin.

The urge to touch him was strong. He's practically a stranger, she reminded herself. And reminded herself also that they were there under horrible circumstances which weren't the best setting for romance. Not to mention the fact that her children were asleep just a few feet away with the connecting door still ajar.

She considered the best way to get out of the bed, but when she tried to ease from under his arm, Joe snuffled an irritated sound and tightened his arm around her. She held her breath and prayed he wouldn't awaken and discover their intimate proximity. Funny that the static of the TV hadn't awakened him. He must have been really tired. But then, he'd done all the driving. She spotted the TV remote on the bed between their bodies. She eased her hand out until she was able to clasp it and then struck the off button with her thumb.

The room fell into darkness except for the merest hint of light from the foyer on the other side of the wall in the other room. Joe's chest moved as he sighed and Kate waited, listening until his breathing evened and she knew he was still asleep. She'd wait until he was really under, and then she'd try again to get out from under that arm.

The waiting didn't take long. In only a few minutes Kate herself was fast asleep.

SHE DREAMED ABOUT an earthquake, about a world gone mad with motion and incredible noise.

She awakened to the feeling of the mattress moving under her, the children jumping up and down on the bed, shouting and laughing and then falling beside her with elbows and knees poking her everywhere.

"Mommy, Joe, wake up, it's breakfast time!"

Mommy. Joe.

Kate opened her eyes and through the flailing arms and jumping bodies of the twins saw that Joe was lying in the bed beside her, his face crinkled with laughter as Robbie jumped astride him and pounded his chest.

She shut her eyes and groaned. Oh, God, how embarrassing was this? She didn't think she could possibly ever open her eyes again, ever look Joe Riley in the face. And what were the children thinking of this unseemly situation.

"Mommy, come on, we want oatmeal."

"Yuck," Robbie screamed. "I hate oatmeal, I want eggs."

Normally Kate would have calmly reminded Robbie that he loved oatmeal and seldom ate eggs, but this was not a normal moment. She clenched teeth, fists and eyelids, and wished she could fall instantly back to sleep and wake up alone on a deserted island. She'd even settle for a cave in the side of a mountain. A prison cell.

"Come on, kids, let's let Mommy sleep a little longer, and we'll go to breakfast."

His morning voice was a deep rumble that Kate could feel right in the pit of her stomach.

The bed bounced again as the three of them got up. Kate peeked through slitted eyes to watch as Joe herded them into the other room to get dressed. Joe was wearing a T-shirt and boxer shorts, and she saw that he had the firm thighs and strong legs of an athlete. She stifled another groan as she thought about those legs up against hers during the night.

Despite the inevitable noise the twins made as they chattered, argued and tried to keep their voices to a whispered roar, Kate was able to drift back to sleep, and the next time she awakened, Joe was leaning over her, murmuring her name and touching her shoulder.

"Kate, it's time to head out," he said.

She sat up, alarmed by the quiet.

"Where are the kids?"

"Outside. There's a picnic table out there and the waitress gave them crayons and a stack of paper place mats to draw on."

"Oh." She sat on the edge of the bed and rubbed her eyes.

"Here." Joe handed her a plastic cup, the aroma of fresh coffee wafting from it. "I brought you some doughnuts, too."

Kate shook her head. "Thank you. Maybe I'll have one in the car. I have to…" She gestured toward the bathroom.

Joe nodded. "Sure. I'll be outside with the twins. We packed our stuff and it's in the car, so you only have to grab your own."

Kate sat a moment, sipping the hot brew and waiting for her mind to catch up with her body. The children hadn't reacted at all to finding her in bed with Joe. They were only six, maybe too young to see anything unusual in that. She'd often thought that one of the great advantages of raising children in small towns was that they weren't as sophisticated as city children, didn't grow up as fast.

Joe had certainly handled the whole thing with aplomb.

Was she the only one who was disturbed by it? And what did that say about her? She wasn't usually prudish, or uptight. And after all, nothing had happened. She wondered how likely it was that a man and woman could share a bed all night and nothing happen. Unless the woman just didn't appeal to the man. Unless he just didn't see her as sexy.

Was that the problem?

She jumped up from the bed and rushed into the other room, refusing to dwell on that last wicked thought…and the way it disturbed her.

She was dressed and packed in record time.

The sun was bright, the sky cloudless, the air soft

and warm. Another beautiful day, she saw when she came out of the motel room. She set her bag down and scanned the grassy area surrounding the motel complex.

The children were busy at their drawings while Joe sat atop the table watching them, his feet on the bench, his head bent as he listened to what they were saying.

They looked like an ordinary family. To the casual passerby, they could be any family on vacation, in no particular hurry to get to their destination, just enjoying the weather and their closeness.

The traffic on the highway beyond the frontage road was heavy, and as cars whizzed past, Kate realized that any one of those cars could be bringing danger to her and to the children.

Despite the warm temperature, a chill moved up Kate's spine and cooled her skin. She ran toward Joe and the children.

"I'm ready. Let's go!"

Joe looked up, a smile on his face, as the twins began to protest that they hadn't finished their pictures.

"You can finish them in the car," Kate said, already snatching up crayons and paper.

"Mo-om! You're crinkling my draw—"

"Ash, we don't have time to dawdle. Let's go."

The twins' mutual look of indignant hurt and Joe's openmouthed stare wrenched at her, but her sudden, inexplicable anxiety took precedence. "Let's just go," she urged.

Joe slipped down from the table and helped the twins gather up their art materials, talking calmly and cheerfully to them as he shepherded them to the car.

Kate got in the front seat as Joe put her bag in the trunk. In the back seat the twins buckled their seat belts without being reminded. The doughnuts sat on the dashboard, grease spots already forming on the white bag.

She wanted to apologize to the children, but the lump was back in her throat, and anyway, she couldn't think what she could say that wouldn't alarm them.

Joe got into the car and started the ignition.

They were all quiet as Joe eased the car into the stream of traffic and continued south on the highway. The children didn't ask where they were going and neither did Kate.

Her mind was frenziedly trying to formulate a plan. They couldn't just take off for parts unknown indefinitely. She had a job, a house, responsibilities. The twins need their home, the roots she'd so carefully planted for them.

She glanced over at Joe, saw the tight set of his jaw, the way his hands clenched the wheel. What did she really know about this man? Only what he'd told her. And that hadn't amounted to much, she realized.

He'd said he wanted to help them, get them away from danger.

But he could, as easily, be driving them right into the danger she thought she was fleeing.

Chapter Seven

Joe used the rearview mirror to monitor the children in the back seat. He didn't like their stillness; it felt unnatural. Kate, too, was staring out of her window as if preoccupied by the passing scenery.

He cleared his throat. "Anybody want to play license plates?"

Nobody spoke.

"How about 'I spy'?"

Again, no answer.

He felt helpless, didn't know how to break through their silence. He gave Kate a sideways glance, hoping she'd at least come out of her reverie. He was still wondering what had happened to make her so jumpy back at the motel, what had made her so desperate to leave and in such a rush. He'd never heard her snap at the children like that.

It dawned on him what was eating at the twins. They were mad at their mom. If that's what it was, they were sure stubborn little rug rats, hanging on to their anger for this long.

He stifled a grin. A road sign on his right announced a food stop at the next ramp exit, listing five different fast-food places.

Without a word, he took the off-ramp and headed for the familiar golden arch.

"Why are we stopping?"

Ah, so something finally brought Kate around.

He ignored her question and pulled into a parking space.

"We just ate, Joe," Ashleigh said.

"You didn't have ice cream, did you?"

"Yay, ice cream! I want chocolate," Robbie yelled.

"Me, too. I want chocolate, Joe," Ashleigh chimed in.

Joe grinned at Kate. "They agreed on something. Yay!" he said softly.

Joe gave them a couple of dollars and sent them in to get the treats.

The minute they were out of the car, Joe turned to Kate.

"All right, Kate, let's have it. What's wrong?"

Kate frowned. "You don't know where you're going, do you?"

Joe shrugged. "The idea was to get you away from Lake George. What difference does it make where we go?"

"And how long do you plan to drive aimlessly? How long before I can return to my job and take my kids back to their home?"

Joe didn't have an answer, hadn't thought that far ahead.

"You don't even have a plan, do you?" she accused.

"A plan? Well, no, not exactly a plan."

Kate folded her arms across her chest and glared at him. "I can't afford to spend my life on the run, Riley, so if you don't have a plan, it looks like I'll have to make one."

"Okay. You make one."

The glare became a look of surprise. She recovered quickly. "Okay. I will."

Joe imitated her stance, folding his own arms as he waited. And waited.

"Well?"

"Well, okay."

"You don't have one, either, do you?"

Kate put her hands over her face and shuddered. "I don't want to give up my life, the children's life. I don't want to start over," she wailed.

Joe didn't hesitate. He pulled her over and put his arms around her. "Don't get upset, Kate. We'll think of something."

"Like what?"

She laid her head against his chest, enjoying the feel of his physical strength, the soapy smell of his recent shower, the man fragrance that she recalled from waking in his bed. She wanted to trust him. Had to trust him. There was no one else.

"Monica must have said something that would give us a clue to what was going on. If we could work that out, we might be able to determine our next move."

Kate shook her head impatiently. "She didn't say anything that I haven't already told…"

She jerked back, pulling out of his arms.

"What? You remembered something?"

Kate nodded, her eyes wide. "I didn't tell you everything. I didn't tell you about the key."

"What key?"

She told him about Monica telling her she'd taped a key under the shelf in her bedroom closet and that Kate was to get it and take it with her.

"When I realized I'd forgotten it, it was too late to

go back for it. Those guys jumped out of a car and ran into the building, and I knew they were the ones Monica wanted me to get away from.''

''So as far as you know, the key is still there?''

She hadn't thought of that. ''Do you think? After all this time?''

Joe stared out the windshield, drumming his fingers on the steering wheel. ''How often do you think anyone removes a shelf from a closet? I don't think even professional painters do that.'' He turned back to Kate, his face alight with optimism. ''Kate, if we can get our hands on that key, we might be able to...''

A terrible scream rent the air, shocking both Kate and Joe into leaping from their respective doors. Robbie's shouts were almost as loud as Ashleigh's screams, and Joe and Kate tore around the building, following the sounds.

People were rushing out of the building as Kate ran to her children. At the edge of the lot a car spun its wheels, screeched brakes, and then spit gravel as it made a U-turn and drove off at top speed.

A crowd had gathered around the children as both of them were yelling about the bad man who tried to make them get in his car. There were two chocolate cones lying in the dirt nearby.

Joe already had Ashleigh in his arms, and Kate snatched Robbie to her and held on for dear life.

''Somebody call the cops,'' one of the onlookers yelled. The manager came out of the back door, his apron swinging around his legs. ''I already did,'' he assured them.

''Ash,'' Joe said, putting her down and kneeling in front of her, ''can you tell us what happened?''

Ashleigh gulped and nodded. Kate could see she was

fighting back tears. "We came out the wrong door. I told Robbie…"

"I made a mistake, Mommy," Robbie admitted, snuggling his head against Kate's shoulder. She could feel the shudders racking his body. Or was that her own body shaking? She thought she might hear the sound of her children screaming in every dream she had from now on.

"It's okay, hon, we all make mistakes." She rubbed his back and looked over his head to give Joe a grim smile.

"So you came out the wrong door. Then what, honey?" Joe asked, prodding the little girl.

"We was gonna sit at that table." Sniffling, she pointed toward a picnic table on a patch of grass. "Just for a minute, and eat our ice cream. Then the car with the bad man came and he got out and told us we was supposed to come with him."

"I told him we never are supposed to get in cars with strangers, Mommy," Robbie interjected, leaning back to look right into Kate's face, his expression righteous with indignation.

"Exactly right, sweetie," Kate congratulated him.

"Yeah," Ashleigh said, "he did. But the bad man grabbed my arm." Ashleigh's face grew red with indignation. "He made me drop my ice cream!" she yelled.

"Me, too. I dropped mine, too," Robbie yelled louder.

"I'll buy you another cone. You can have all the ice cream you want," Joe promised, trying to head off one of their competitive bouts. "What happened then?"

"The lady ossifer said scream," Ashleigh said, nodding her head. "I want a swirly this time."

Joe looked helplessly at Kate.

Kate exhaled. "They had a female police officer visit them in kindergarten. She gave them guidelines for what to do if a stranger approached any of them."

"So we did," Robbie said, squirming to get free of Kate's embrace. "We screamed and screamed and the bad man got scared and ran away in his car."

The siren that had been a distant signal from the highway became a raucous blare as a patrol car pulled into the lot and two cops jumped out and ran toward the crowd.

After another run-through from the children, one of the officers asked if they could describe the car.

"It was great big," Robbie said, "and scary."

"It was a Chevy Blazer," Ashleigh said succinctly, "and it was blue and white and it had a spare tire on the back."

There wasn't a sound beyond the distant hum of the traffic on the highway, as everyone but Kate gaped at the little girl.

One of the policemen broke the awed silence when he turned to Kate and said, "Could she be right, ma'am?"

Kate nodded. "Ash loves anything on wheels. If she says it was a Blazer, it was."

Some of the crowd chimed in that they'd seen a blue-and-white Blazer take off right after they responded to the children's screams.

The other officer ran over to the patrol car and used the police radio to make a report and have the highway patrol alerted.

"Sir—" the other man addressed Joe "—would you mind following us to the police station in town to file a report?"

Joe and Kate exchanged a glance and Kate nodded.

"We need our ice cream first," Robbie reminded the adults.

"So you do," the manager said, laughing. "I'll go get them for you."

He was back in two minutes and refused Joe's offer of money. "Listen, I hope you don't hold this against us. Honestly, we've never had anything like that happen here before."

Kate reassured him that they had no intention of blaming his establishment, thanked him again for the cones and herded the children into the car.

They spoke in low tones as they followed the patrol car.

"Most likely a random attempt," Joe said, looking over his shoulder to make sure the children hadn't heard him. They were busy with their ice cream.

Kate agreed. "We couldn't have been followed."

"I think I would have noticed. So, what about the cops?"

Kate glanced back at the children and reached in her purse for napkins.

"You're dripping, Ash. Try not to get any on the seat."

She turned back to Joe and lowered her voice. "There isn't any need to say anything, is there?"

Joe kept his gaze on the patrol car and signaled a right turn when it did.

"No. I think all they want is an official report— maybe a description from the kids. Shouldn't take too long."

"And then?"

Joe's voice was almost a whisper. "And then I think we work out a plan to find that key."

An hour later they were back on the road, this time heading south. The children, worn out from their adventure and the excitement of visiting a real police station, answering questions and being congratulated by all the personnel there for their smart, quick thinking, fell asleep only minutes after they got back on the highway.

Joe's hand snaked out and caught and held Kate's. "You okay, hon?"

Kate clung to his hand, grateful for his concern, but not sure how she felt about the casual term of affection.

"I don't think I'll ever close my eyes without hearing the children's screams. And I was a nervous wreck the whole time we were at the police station, thinking someone was suddenly going to remember my… Monica's name, from back when all that was on the news."

Joe glanced in the rearview mirror and then in both side mirrors. He didn't expect to have a tail, but it didn't hurt to stay alert.

"It was a long time ago. I doubt it would have been as big a deal out here in the boonies. Still, it was a relief to get out of there."

"What now, Joe?"

"Manhattan."

Kate jerked around. "You've got to be kidding. That's walking right into the lion's mouth!"

Joe shook his head. "I don't think so. First of all, nobody is going to be expecting us to show up there. And second, there's no better place to go underground than in a big city. And third, that's where the key is."

"What about the children? We can't take them into a dangerous situation. And we sure can't take them with us while we're looking for the key."

"Hotels, the good ones, have baby-sitting services, don't they?"

"Hotels? I guess…yes. But are we really going to check into a big hotel?"

"Yup." Joe signaled and moved into the fast lane, passing an elderly man in an old car who seemed uncertain about where he was and how fast he wanted to go.

"I'm borrowing a page from your book, Kate. You said you stopped because you thought whoever was after you would run right past, not expecting you to stop. Well, nobody is going to expect us to march right back to the scene of the crime, so to speak, and make ourselves as visible as tourists."

Kate liked it that he referred to her past methods with such approval, and the more she thought about it, the more sense it made. Nobody who was after them would expect them to be right in their midst, right under their noses.

They drove straight through and arrived in the city at dusk. They'd stopped for an early dinner and Joe had called a midtown hotel to make a reservation for a two-bedroom suite with its own living room. He didn't know how long all this was going to take, and he couldn't see the twins cooped up in a bedroom for any length of time.

As they settled in, readying the children for bed, Kate was gratified to discover that the twins seemed to be suffering no residual trauma from their early-morning incident with the "bad man."

As she dried Robbie and got him into his pajamas after his bath, she could hear Ashleigh in the bedroom, telling Joe some long, convoluted story about how one of her kindergarten classmates had lost his first tooth and how the tooth fairy made a mistake and went to the wrong house. Joe's laughter brought an unexpected lurch to her stomach, a slight tremor to her hands.

"Whatsa matter, Mommy?" Robbie asked when her fingers refused to connect the button with the button-hole.

She tousled his damp curls and hugged him. "Not a thing, bucko. I'm just a little tired from the long trip."

"How come we came to New York, Mom? I thought we were going on vacation."

Kate finished buttoning the pajama top and bent to let the water out of the tub. "People come to New York for vacations all the time, Robbie. Don't you think a big, exciting city is a good place to visit? There's tons to do here."

"Kin we go on the Statue of Liberty ride?"

Kate laughed as she kneeled to gather up wet towels and cast-off clothing. "It's not a ride, sweetie, but, yes, I guess we can go out to see it. You have to go on a boat to see it. You'll like that, I know."

Joe had Ashleigh tucked in and was looking in the children's bag for a bedtime book. Robbie ran into the bedroom and jumped on his back. "Joe, we're going on the Statue of Liberty. Yay!"

"We are, huh?" Joe laughed and wrestled the little boy down and tossed him on the bed. "But right now you're going on the sleep train." He sat on the edge of the bed and made a pull-down motion with his fist. "All aboa-oared. Whoo-whoo!"

Kate smiled at the sound of the children's laughter and stuffed the soiled clothing into a plastic bag. Joe was so good with kids. It was too bad he had none of his own. But as she headed back into the bathroom she chided herself for the thought. Joe was still a young man. He had plenty of time to have children.

She put the cap back on the toothpaste tube and rinsed the twins' brushes. When she raised her head, she caught her reflection in the mirror, startled by her own unfamiliar image. She leaned forward and brushed her fingers over the shadows beneath her eyes. "I don't transplant well," she muttered, wishing desperately that she was about to go into her own bedroom back in Lake George. Or maybe it wasn't so much being away from home as it was the sense of doom that hung over her. Hard as she'd tried to convince Joe that Wilkins's murder hadn't necessarily been connected to his investigation of Monica's death, she knew at heart it was the most likely explanation.

She moved the twins' little toiletries bag into a corner of the counter and spotted the gift basket the hotel provided for guests. Picking up one of the small bottles, she saw by the label that it was a bubble bath. The idea of a long, luxurious bath, thick with creamy suds, had great appeal. She peeked into the bedroom and saw that Joe was reading to the twins.

Quietly closing the door, she bent to close the drain on the tub and started the water running over the splash of bubble bath.

Fragrant steam rose as she slid into the lather-silkened water, and Kate sighed her pleasure aloud.

At first her thoughts centered on the problem of retrieving Monica's hidden key. Would the super let them into the apartment if they explained what they were looking for? She wondered if the same super ran the building. What was his name? A little man with rough edges who seemed more country than city. Sarter, Sander, Selmos? No.

She remembered a few times when he'd helped her down the stairs with the twin stroller and how he always bent to chuck the babies under their chins and to babble baby noises at them. Monica had called him a displaced redneck, but she'd appreciated that he was one of the few supers in the city who actually did his job with diligence and was always polite, in his surly way, to the tenants. Mr. Santos. That was it.

As Kate raised her fist in triumph, clumps of bubbles slid down her arm and flew into her face. She laughed and grabbed a towel off the rack to dry her eyes.

She lay back, recalling more about Mr. Santos. If the apartment was currently rented, there was no way the super would ever let them in. She pondered the idea of just ringing the bell and asking the tenant of 2A to let them in to look under the shelf for the key, and then scoffed aloud at her foolish fantasy. No way was any New Yorker going to buzz them up, let alone invite two strangers into the apartment to explore a closet. Paranoia was a requirement for citizenship in the city. They probably put a drug to ensure it into the city water supply. She was probably steeping in it right this moment.

She smiled, closed her eyes and slid down into the tub until only her face was above water.

They'd have to break in.

Kate bolted upright, her eyes flying open, her body rigid with horror. What a concept! Breaking and entering to discover a key that might very well unlock some kind of evidence that would prove Monica, once her best friend, her children's birth mother, guilty of a crime. And committing a crime in the process. She and Joe could well end up in jail.

Oh, that would look great for the twins' legacy.

She got out of the tub and reached for the terry robe that hung on the door. So what alternative did that leave for getting that key? Or maybe the key wasn't the only means of finding out what they needed to know.

She sat on the edge of the tub and toweled her legs. Monica's body had been found in the alley behind the Kismet Club, the place where Monica had performed. And she'd been involved, somewhat, with the owner, Springer. Joe told her that Wilkins had been able to find out nothing from Springer, but that didn't mean he didn't know anything. Maybe Springer would be more open with a woman. With her. If she played on his sympathy, pointing out that she was in danger, that the children could come to harm…

The children.

She held the towel to her mouth and stared at her face in the mirror. Could Don Springer be the children's father? And if he was their father, wouldn't he be willing to do anything to make sure they were safe? The more she thought about it, the more likely the prospect seemed.

Excitement revved, and she fumbled the door open and rushed into the bedroom to tell Joe.

Her breath caught in her throat, clogging the words she was about to prattle in her excitement.

They were all three asleep—the children on their pillows, Joe at their feet, the open book clutched against his chest. A touching tableau of a family.

For a moment she stood there, considering the idea of waking Joe, sending him into his own room, to his own bed. She slipped the book from his hands and set it on the nightstand. A shock of Joe's hair had fallen forward over one eyebrow, and Kate wanted to reach out and brush it back. She clenched her fists at her sides and bit her lip.

Her libido was in overdrive these days, ever since she'd first laid eyes on Joe Riley. If she wasn't careful, she'd wind up in a situation far more dangerous than the one she was running from. A person could only die once, but living with disappointment and heartache could last an entire lifetime.

She turned and pulled the spread off the second bed and gently covered Joe with it. Then she went back to the other bed and slipped beneath the covers.

Kate lay awake for a few minutes, watching Joe sleep and remembering the feeling of sharing a bed with him the night before. There was something cozy about all of them sleeping in the same room tonight. Like a real family. It made her think about the times she'd envied women who had a man to share the burdens and the joys with; women like her friend Marybeth. Someday, she thought as her eyelids drifted down.

A flash of clarity startled her and her eyes popped open. If Springer had any thought he was the children's father, wouldn't he have been the one looking for them? And if that were so, wouldn't it be foolhardy to confront him?

But she wouldn't be alone, she'd have Joe with her. Joe, who was big and strong and who made her feel safe and protected. A flush of warmth cocooned her and in minutes she was asleep.

Joe felt the cover falling over him and held his breath, afraid to let Kate know he had awakened. He watched from under his eyelashes as she climbed into the other bed and adjusted her pillow under her cheek. He wasn't sure, but he thought she was staring straight at him and he held himself as still as possible. When she fell asleep, he sensed it, and he lifted himself carefully off the children's bed.

He went to the other bed and stood, looking down at Kate, her hair a mass of flames against the white pillow, her breasts rising and falling beneath the sheet in rhythm with her breathing.

I could slip in beside her and I'll bet she wouldn't awaken, he thought. He remembered the way she'd curled toward him in her sleep...was it only last night? He took a step forward. If she awakened, would she reach for him instinctively or would she scream in terror and waken the twins?

Reminded that the children were there, just two feet away, was what brought him to his senses. With regret and a touch of relief, he left the room for his own bedroom, his own cold, empty bed.

Chapter Eight

In the morning, after a riotous breakfast at the table in the living room of the suite, Kate interviewed a woman from the baby-sitter service.

After brief introductions, Joe and the twins left to swim in the hotel pool, leaving Kate and Mrs. Milkamp to get acquainted. Kate poured coffee for the prospective baby-sitter and studied the woman with a practiced eye.

Donna Milkamp was in her middle fifties, a faded blonde with a neat appearance and a soft-spoken manner. Kate liked the way the woman's brown eyes twinkled and the easy way she answered questions.

"You don't sound like a New Yorker, Mrs. Milkamp," Kate said.

The older woman chuckled. "Ohio. Logan, Ohio. Can you imagine little Donna Swarth Milkamp in the Big Apple after fifty-three years living in a place the size of Logan?"

Kate had no idea of the size of Logan, but she suspected it was probably much like Lake George.

"Why did you come to New York?" she asked, finding herself really interested.

"Oh, my husband got this big promotion at the insurance company he works for and it meant moving to headquarters. You can imagine the reaction of all our friends and family. I admit, the idea was a little scary at first, with all you see on TV and all, but it's been better than we expected. I signed up at the agency, and Dale, that's my husband, he works long hours now, so we're both too busy to miss home. And we've seen every single musical comedy on Broadway this season. Just like tourists,'' she concluded with a proud giggle.

"Do you have children of your own, Mrs. Milkamp?''

"Call me Donna.'' The woman sipped from her cup and nodded her head. "Three. Two girls and a boy. All grown up so fast. 'Course now my husband and I have more time for each other.'' She looked pensive and added, almost under her breath, "When he's not working, that is.''

Her cheerful expression quickly restored itself.

"Your husband is so good with the children. And very handsome. No wonder the kids are so adorable. They look just like him. 'Cept for the dark hair, of course.'' She peered at Kate's red curls.

"You'd think they'd have inherited all that gorgeous red hair of yours. Too bad. No telling about genes, though, right?''

Kate stared at the other woman. Did the twins really look like Joe? She'd suspected that Springer was their father, but wasn't it just as likely that Joe…?

But, no! She brushed the thought away, finding it too awful to accept. Mrs. Milkamp was the kind of person who made that kind of comment off-handedly, and proof of that was the way she'd also assumed Joe was Kate's husband.

Well, Kate could set that straight immediately.

"He's just a very close friend who is…well, we have business together in the city and…" She realized she was blushing. She jerked her arm in the direction of the adjoining room. "That's Joe's room. The children and I are in the other bedroom."

"Oh, my," the older woman wailed. "I'm sorry if I was out of line or anything…."

"It's all right, really. I just thought you should know, for the record," Kate said, anxious to put the sitter back at ease. Fortunately the woman was cheerful by nature and soon they were chatting like old friends.

"There's something else you should know, Mrs… um, Donna. A man approached the children when we were at McDonalds and although I'm sure it was a random attempt, I'd like you to be sure to keep the children close by whenever you take them out of the hotel."

The older woman nodded. "No need to remind me of that," she said, "I know about the dangers here in the city."

Kate looked thoughtful. "You know, we were practically out in the country when that happened and because we live in a small town, it never occurred to me that the twins couldn't go into a fast food place by themselves with Joe and I waiting for them right outside the door."

"Tsk, tsk." Now Donna was shaking her head, her face puckered with disgust. "Those perverts are everywhere nowadays, I guess. Nobody's safe anymore. Well, don't you worry, I'll keep the babes right up under my wing."

Their discussion was interrupted as Joe and the kids came barreling into the room laughing, shivering and dripping water on the carpet.

Donna had no commitments for the day and she pitched right in, helping the children get out of their swimsuits, dry off and get dressed. She asked to see their books and toys and soon had them seated at the table wrapped up in a board game, which brought so much laughter and giggles that Kate was afraid some other hotel guest might complain to the management about the noise coming from their suite.

When Donna left at four, with an agreement to return the next morning at ten, the twins insisted on giving her goodbye hugs and Kate knew she was going to work out fine. With that settled, she and Joe would be able to plan an agenda for retrieving the key.

They took the children to Central Park to the petting zoo and ate spaghetti at an Italian restaurant near the hotel, which caused great hilarity as the twins and Joe tried to outdo each other slurping long strands of pasta off their forks. Kate pretended to be disgusted by their behavior and threatened to move by herself to another table, which only incited them to more laughter and silliness. She ended up joining in, despite her I'm-the-only-grown-up-here protestations.

Afterward Joe led the way along streets of shops until they came to FAO Schwartz. The twins' eyes got big as saucers when they peered in the windows of the huge toy store. "It's so cool," Ashleigh breathed.

"Totally awesome," Robbie said with a sigh.

"They have plenty of toys and games," Kate said when Joe suggested they go inside. "I try to keep presents to a minimum, like birthdays and Christmas, so they won't get spoiled."

"They aren't spoiled," Joe insisted, "and I don't think one little toy each will do much harm."

She liked it that he didn't think the kids were

spoiled. It suggested he thought she was doing a good job raising them.

Joe took advantage of her softened mood and herded them all ahead of him through the revolving doors.

The children were awed enough to behave with more decorum than usual. It was Joe she had to pull away from electric trains, computerized games and child-size musical instruments. When he wound up half a dozen mechanical monkeys and had them bobbing all over the aisle to the twins' delight, Kate raised her voice and threatened that if he touched one more thing they were leaving immediately.

Robbie picked out a stuffed kangaroo with a baby roo in its pocket, and Ashleigh, ever the competitor, selected the game of Trouble, chattering all the way back to the hotel about how she was going to beat everyone when they played.

But her head began to nod during the first game and Robbie kept rubbing his eyes and yawning. Kate and Joe exchanged a mutual nod, each of them picking up a child, and carried them to the bedroom. They were asleep before Kate had the covers pulled up to their chins.

Joe had the living room lights turned out, save for a single lamp on the dining table, when she returned to the living room. Instead of the TV, he'd turned on the radio, and Kate smiled as she recognized the newest song by Clint Black.

"Care for a glass of wine?" Joe held the bottle aloft and grinned at her. "Compliments of the minibar."

"It's not free, you know," Kate warned.

"Nothing is, these days." Joe was already opening the bottle.

Curiosity got the better of good manners. "You're a

regular big spender, Riley. Did you come into an inheritance, win the lottery?'' She blushed, wondering if she sounded as suspicious to his ears as she did to her own.

Joe handed her a glass of wine and strolled over to the couch. ''There's not much to spend your money on in the desert. Company perks provided living quarters and meals, so I was able to bank most of my paychecks during the seven years I was over there.'' He leaned into the corner of the couch and crossed the ankle of his right leg over the knee of his left.

His face creased with an expression she could only read as fatigue, but she suspected there was something more there. She put her glass down on the coffee table and sat beside him.

''Joe, how did you let yourself get so caught up in all this? I mean, what do you get out of it?''

Joe rubbed his forehead, a gesture she was becoming familiar with, and closed his eyes briefly. When he opened them she could see a glint of fervor there.

''You know, I love my work. I love the adventure of it, the science of it, the basic order of it.'' He paused and shook his head. ''But after seven years of field work, I came back feeling empty. Like I'd been on a deserted island for all that time.'' He chuckled softly. ''At first I thought it was probably about the difference in culture—Arabia was pretty arid for an American, in more ways than just the deserts. But I wasn't back twenty-four hours before I realized it had nothing to do with where I'd been or where I was now—it was more about *who* I am.

''And then I understood that I'd never really been involved with anyone in my whole life. Oh, I'd had affairs, friends, colleagues with whom I shared my work. But I never got inside anyone, never let anyone get inside me.''

Kate realized she'd been holding her breath. She let it out in a long, gusty sigh and nodded.

Joe gave her a searching look and returned the nod as he saw understanding in her eyes.

''I don't know if it was meeting Matt Wilkins, or learning about Monica's death or...'' He stopped and shook his head. He wanted to tell her about the strange connection he'd felt the first time their eyes met when he passed her in that café window, but he couldn't. There were still too many unanswered questions between them.

Anne Murray was singing something sweet and slow on the radio.

On impulse, Kate stood up and held out her hand. ''Dance with me, Joe?''

She fit in his arms just the way she knew she would, their steps in perfect sync, as if they'd danced together for years.

She'd anticipated, almost feared, a sexual response, but found instead that what she felt was comfort, both a giving and receiving of it. Something very like friendship, trust.

They danced in silence until the song ended and then exchanged a smile, still holding each other. Kate had to tilt her head a little to look up into his face.

''You're a good dancer, Riley.''

''A little rusty, but I guess it's like riding a bike.''

She knew she should let go, step out of his arms. She could feel the heat of his skin beneath his shirt, the power of his shoulder muscles where her hand touched him.

"Didn't you date, go out dancing, while you were in Arabia?" She cleared her throat.

He looked down into her face and noticed for the first time that she had a tiny mole near the corner of her top lip. "Yeah, a little." His voice suddenly seemed to clog in his throat. "What's that song?" he asked, tilting his head toward the radio.

"One of my favorites," she murmured as he began to move in a slow circle. "But I can't for the life of me name the song or the artist."

Joe smiled. "I like it," he said, and pulled her closer.

She followed his lead, refitting herself to his body and drifting into the dance. Very comfortable, she thought, appreciating the warmth. She brushed the back of her hand across her forehead, feeling the dampness there. Maybe a little too warm.

Joe inhaled the fragrance of Kate's hair as it caressed his chin, and he tightened his hand on her waist. "You smell wonderful," he whispered. "Like vanilla and lemons and spices."

"You make me sound like a pound cake," Kate said, laughing softly.

"No, a pound cake is too plain. You're richer, more exotic…like a brandied fruitcake."

She stopped dancing. Her laugh became full-blown. "In some circles it would be considered an insult to be called a fruitcake, Riley."

Joe grinned. "I guess my ability to compliment a beautiful woman has grown rusty as well." He twined a wisp of her hair around his finger and his expression sobered.

"You have a very strange effect on me, Kate." He tilted his head toward her.

Kate swallowed and felt the smile on her face stiffen.

He was going to kiss her. She tried to tell herself she didn't want it, wouldn't allow it, but her head had already tilted to meet his and her hands were moving up his arms as if they had a will of their own.

The kiss was the merest whisper of greeting, like the nods between strangers passing in the street, a warm rustling of air around her lips. Kate held her breath and waited for Joe's lips to return to hers, to stake a positive claim.

Instead, he withdrew, his shoulders moving out from under her grasp. Her eyes drifted open and she stumbled slightly without the support of his hands at her waist.

"Joe?"

"I'm sorry, Kate. I guess I lost my sanity for a minute there."

"No, I didn't…"

"We need to keep focused," Joe said, going to the radio and turning it off. The silence hung between them. Kate returned to the couch, reaching for her drink as she sat down.

She should be grateful that he'd had the sense to back off. She was. Or she would be once she came to her own senses and stopped trembling. She took a hefty swallow of the wine.

"So where do we start?" she asked when she could trust her voice.

"How well did you know the super at the brownstone?" Joe asked.

"Well enough so I think he'd remember me, if it's still Mr. Santos," she said.

"Good. Then I think I know how we can get into that apartment."

"Without breaking any laws?" Kate asked, her mouth twisted wryly.

"Well...I can't promise that. It would help if the apartment isn't currently rented."

"And if it is?"

Joe avoided her gaze by leaning forward to pick up his own glass of wine.

"Then we may have to break a few laws." He faced her then. "And make damned sure we don't get caught."

"Mother of two found guilty of breaking and entering," Kate murmured.

"What was that?"

"Headlines."

Joe chuckled. "Bonnie and Clyde."

"I'm glad your sense of humor is still working."

He ignored that.

"If the apartment happens to be vacant, we've got no problem other than getting into the building. If it is, we're going to have to get creative in order to get the master key."

"Does having the master key mean it isn't breaking and entering?"

"No, but it makes getting in easier."

They discussed various methods and finally came up with a plan they thought would work, given that Mr. Santos was still super at the brownstone. Kate felt rather optimistic when Joe described the man he'd met and talked with.

"That sounds like Santos," she agreed.

"Okay, then we'll go over there in the morning after Donna gets here. Want any more of this?" He waved the wine bottle.

"No. Thanks. I think I'll get to bed."

Joe nodded. "Go ahead. I'll straighten up and get the lights."

Kate hesitated at the door to her room. "Joe, about before…"

"Don't, Kate!" Joe interrupted. "It would have been a mistake."

Kate nodded and opened the door without looking back. Why didn't she feel convinced that he was right?

THE SUPER DIDN'T INVITE them in; he just stood in the door of his apartment, glaring at Kate.

"I thought you'd disappeared off the face of the earth," the little man said, peering up at Kate. "Seems like you'da let a body know you was leavin' or somethin'. Caused me a lotta trouble, I can tell ya."

"I'm so sorry, Mr. Santos," Kate said, surprised that she was actually feeling shame. She recalled that Monica always said Santos made her feel as if she were still eight years old, still in pigtails, when he found reason to chastise her about anything. He did a lot of that, Kate remembered, considering himself an expert on everything from child-raising to politics.

"You're the guy was here coupla weeks back," the super accused Joe, ignoring Kate's apology.

His glance moved from Joe to Kate and back again. "You two together?" His tone was heavy with suspicion.

"We…uh, we wondered if my old apartment was vacant, Mr. Santos," Kate said.

The super snickered at the idea. "Not hardly. This area's prime. Anyhow, can't see the management lettin' you have another shot at the property," he scolded, "seein' as how you left without notice."

"Is the tenant around?" Joe asked, surreptitiously

rubbing Kate's back to keep her from snapping at the super.

"Works." He peered at Joe and frowned. "Seems like a healthy young feller like you'd be to work yourself this time a day."

"I work nights," Joe said, straight-faced. It worked to derail whatever lecture Santos was gearing up for. "Think the guy would be home tonight?" he asked.

"Dunno what the tenants do at night. Most of 'em run around half the night. Don't know what they find out there to keep 'em so busy. Got my own business to tend to."

Kate felt Joe nudge the small of her back. It was her cue.

"Uh, Mr. Santos, would it be too much trouble to ask to use your phone before we leave? Mr. Riley needs to make an appointment with a Realtor about another apartment."

"Local?" The suspicion was back on the super's face.

"Absolutely," Joe assured him.

The man hesitated and Kate hoped her expression conveyed trustworthiness and female helplessness.

"Ain't a public phone booth here, ya know," the man muttered, but he stepped back to let Joe enter the apartment.

"I'll wait here, Joe," Kate called out.

As soon as the two men left the doorway, she peeked in, looking around the edge of the doorjamb. Sure enough, the peg board with tools and the master keys to all the apartments was still nailed up on the wall as she remembered.

She waited until she heard the sound of Joe punching in the numbers, and then she began to cough, pushing the door slightly more ajar so Santos would be sure to hear her. When she'd worked up a good spasm, bordering on choking, she called out to him.

"Mr....Mr. Sa-Santos. Please." Her voice was just raspy enough to be convincing and she was doubled over coughing into her closed fist.

Santos returned to the door. "Pl-please. Could I have...water?"

She heard him grumble as he moved away, and she quickly lifted her head and stepped forward. He had his back to her, and he was headed into the small kitchen beyond the living room. It took her less than 5 seconds to spot the key for 2A, and replace it with the dummy key Joe had picked up at the drugstore. By the time the man returned with half a glass of tepid water, the key was in her jacket pocket.

It took all her determination to swallow the water without gagging, and she handed the glass back with tears running down her face and thanked him.

Joe came up behind Santos, clapped him on the back and thanked him for his kindness. The man grunted and almost slammed the door in their faces when Joe stepped out into the hall.

They were at the outside door when they heard Santos call out to them.

Kate froze, fear sending needles of ice up her spine.

"Some woman came looking for you," he yelled.

Kate and Joe exchanged a look of sheer relief.

"For me?" Kate asked, turning back.

"Yep. Said she was a friend of yours."

"Did she leave a name?"

Santos pulled a cigarette out of his pocket and looked at it before sticking it in the corner of his mouth. He shook his head. "Can't recall."

"What did she look like?"

"Skinny. Blond hair. Too short if you ask me. Women oughta look like women and leave lookin' like a man to the men."

"Was she tall?"

Santos tilted his head, squinting his eyes against the smoke that drifted up from the cigarette. "'Bout your height…mebbe a bit taller."

"Could it have been Terri Maynard?" Kate couldn't think of anyone else among her old friends who fit that description.

"Could be. Can't be sure. Sumpin' like that."

"Did she leave a message?"

"Said to tell you she was wonderin' about you is all."

Kate nodded and was about to turn away.

"Asked too many questions," Santos said.

"What kind of questions?"

"Kind I couldn't answer 'cause you never told no one where you was off to nor if you'd be back, missy."

Kate felt as if she was expected to apologize again, but she decided it wasn't worth the effort. Instead she thanked the man and hurried after Joe.

They went up out into the alley and along the side of the building to the street.

When they were a block from the building, Joe said, "Wilkins mentioned talking to a Terri Maynard. You worked with her, right?"

"Yes. I always meant to keep in touch after HRE was shut down, but before I could do that, Monica…well, you know."

Joe raised his arm to hail a cab. "She live in the city, too?"

Kate's brow creased. "I think she lived right there

in Yonkers. As I recall, I was the only one of the crew who lived in Manhattan.''

The cab drew up to the curb and Joe held the door as Kate climbed inside. When he'd given the cabbie the name of the hotel, Joe turned to Kate.

''So she came all the way into the city to talk to Santos in person after you left.''

Kate stared at Joe. ''I guess that is a little strange.'' She thought about it. ''But maybe she was in the city on some other business and dropped by on a whim as long as she was in town, anyway.'' She smiled, remembering. ''We were pretty good friends, actually. If things hadn't happened the way they did, I would have kept in touch with her.''

Joe shrugged and looked out the window. ''I guess that's possible.''

''What are we going to do now?''

He lowered his voice so the driver wouldn't overhear.

''Let Donna go for the day and ask her to come back tonight.''

''Gosh, what if she's already made plans for tonight and can't sit for us?''

Joe looked thoughtful. ''I guess I'll have to do this alone.''

For some reason the idea of Joe sneaking into the brownstone, going into the apartment alone, made her nervous. She told herself she was concerned for his safety. But a little niggle of doubt played at the back of her mind. At some level, she still didn't entirely trust Joe Riley, and that modicum of uncertainty made her want to keep an eye on him.

''If Donna can't come back, we could always wait and do this tomorrow night,'' she suggested.

Joe shook his head. "I don't think so. It's too dangerous to keep the master key any longer than we have to. If Santos discovers it's gone, there's every chance he'll put it together that we're the ones who took it. I don't fancy showing up there to be met by the cops."

Kate didn't like that scenario, either. She crossed her fingers that Donna would be free that night.

The cab pulled up in front of the hotel just then and Kate waited as Joe paid the fare. As she gazed idly out of the window, past Joe's shoulder, she gasped aloud.

"What?" Joe jerked around to see what was wrong.

Kate stared at the crowd of people moving away from the hotel. She shook her head. "Nothing," she said. "I just thought I saw Terri Maynard. But I must have imagined it. It must be the power of suggestion—because we were just talking about her."

Joe stared at the bobbing heads that moved toward the corner of the block. None were blond. He got out of the cab and offered his hand to help Kate out.

"Imagination can play funny tricks," he agreed, slamming the door of the cab as Kate stepped up to the curb. "Anyway, if it was Maynard, that'd be a hell of a coincidence."

Kate didn't comment, but she looked over her shoulder one last time before stepping through the revolving door into the hotel lobby.

Chapter Nine

"I'm going down to get the paper," Joe said, reaching for his jacket. "Why don't you get the kids ready and I'll meet you down in the lobby."

"You sure you don't mind another day at the zoo?"

Joe laughed. "It could be worse. They could be asking to see *Cats* two days in a row."

Kate grinned. She loved his laugh; it reminded her of the way Robbie laughed, right from the belly. "See you in five." She waved as he went out of the suite.

The door to the bedroom was slightly ajar as Kate approached, her footsteps silenced by the hall runner. She was about to push it open when she heard Robbie said, "Do you love Joe, Ash?"

There was a moment's silence, during which Kate's breath caught in her throat and hung there, her hand frozen over the wood panel.

"Do you?"

"I asked you first."

"I was thinking it first."

"Were not."

"Were, too."

"Okay then. I'll tell you if you'll tell me."

"Okay."

"Okay."

Kate relaxed and smiled. By now they'd probably forgotten what the conversation was supposed to be about. She pushed the door open. The children were sitting cross-legged on the floor in front of the TV, their backs to the door. They were watching a music video channel with the sound muted, a little trick they'd contrived to keep Kate from discovering them watching forbidden videos. Her smile widened; they still hadn't caught on that it was the lyrics she objected to.

"I do love him," Ashleigh pronounced solemnly. "I love him more than anyone. Except Mommy and you." Her dark curls bobbed as she nodded for emphasis.

"Me, too. I love him more than anyone except Mommy and you." Robbie's little bottom bobbed up and down as he squirmed, keeping his eyes focused on the TV, probably embarrassed to be saying something nice to his sister.

Kate's stomach took a nosedive and she stepped back from the open doorway before the children became aware of her presence.

This was something she hadn't anticipated, hadn't prepared herself for; the depth of their attachment to Joe Riley.

They were loving and affectionate by nature, a precious gift from their natural mother, Kate had always suspected, and they gave and received it easily to the people who were constants in their lives. They always remembered the people they loved when they said their prayers at night. Of course, sometimes, when they wanted to delay bedtime, the list grew suspiciously long, but as a general rule, Kate knew they were sincere in their declarations of love.

A week ago, Marybeth would have been first on their

list after Kate and the other twin, with Marybeth's husband, Jon, a close second.

How had they formed such intense feelings for Riley in only a few days? Long days to be sure, and the time Joe had spent with them could certainly qualify as "quality time," but if they already loved him, the feelings were only going to get stronger as the days passed. And then, how would they feel when Joe went right out of their lives? As he surely would. He'd told her he'd been transferred back to New York. But he worked for an oil company as a geologist. The chances were he wouldn't be looking for oil on the island of Manhattan. Sooner or later he'd be sent far afield again and then...

She went back into the living room and sank into a chair. This was one of the reasons she'd been so wary of dating, so careful to keep her social life separate from the twins; to prevent attachments that were going to end up in disappointment for the children. They were too young to endure constant losses. They'd had a major loss at birth when Monica decided to raise them without benefit of a father and again, though they weren't aware of it, when they lost their natural mother.

She rubbed her forehead and then her eyes, the urge to cry a burning sensation behind her lids. If anything happened to her, the loss to the children would be horrific. And here she was, playing detective games with Riley, putting herself right out there where she could easily be targeted for death. What she should have done, she realized, was take the children and run, without Joe Riley, who may well have been responsible for leading the killers right to her doorstep. She'd done it before, successfully, for six years. She could have done it again.

But if Wilkins and Riley had found her so easily this time, what would prevent someone else finding her? For a moment she had a vision of spotting Terri Maynard outside the hotel entrance. "And what's the relevance of that?" she murmured. The relevant thing was that she couldn't spend her life in hiding, couldn't keep the children on the run for the rest of their lives.

"Mommy, are we going to the zoo pretty soon?"

Kate jumped, startled out of her reverie. "I was just coming to get you, Ash. You kids wash your hands and faces and grab your jackets. Joe's waiting downstairs."

Joe was in front of the tobacco stand reading the headlines when the trio got off the elevator. He looked up and watched their approach, and his heart felt as if it had lurched in his chest and then dropped to his stomach. Robbie looked up just then and spotted him.

"Daddy! We're going to the zoo now, Daddy."

Joe blinked and grabbed the counter behind him, a strange vertigo threatening to topple him.

"You okay, sir?" the clerk asked.

Joe. Robbie had called him "Joe," not "Daddy." It had been a weird lapse of his sanity to have imagined the other.

"Joe, are you all right?" Kate came up and put her hand on his arm, her eyes worried as she stared up at him. The children had crowded round, pulling on Joe's hands, jumping up and down and squealing their eagerness to get to the zoo.

"I'm fine," Joe assured her, "just fine."

God, she is so beautiful, he thought, looking down into her face. He had an intense desire to embrace her, to embrace all three of them, to hold them close, keep them safe forever.

"I'm going to feed the seals," Robbie said, yanking Joe's hand to capture his attention. "Mommy said so." Joe swallowed with difficulty and pushed the errant thought out of his mind.

"And I'm going to feed the lions," Ash said.

"You can't feed the lions," Robbie yelled. "She can't, can she, Joe? Lions don't eat fish or peanuts, do they, Joe?"

"No, lions eat little boys and girls," Joe said, and then bent down and roared right into the children's faces as loud as he could. The children screamed and then fell into fits of laughter that still carried traces of fear.

Kate looked around, expecting everyone in the lobby to be glaring disapproval at the noisy family, and found instead that people were smiling, a few even laughing.

"Come on," she said, pretending to be embarrassed, "let's get out of here before we get evicted for creating a scene."

It was at the monkey cages that Kate had her revelation. She thought, later, that it was the kids talking about loving Joe that had brought it to mind, the power of suggestion at work again.

All three of them, Joe and the twins, were making faces at the monkeys, getting a big kick out of the monkeys' screeching reactions. Kate looked at the three of them, with their fingers in their ears, wagging their hands, their faces scrunched up, and her stomach suddenly began to do flips and rolls as if she were aboard a ship on a storm-tossed sea.

She clung to the fence, her fingers curled around the chains, afraid her legs wouldn't hold her up.

Could it be? It would certainly explain Joe Riley hiring a private detective to locate her and the twins.

It would justify the children's feelings toward him; that at some primal level they recognized their blood tie to him.

"And he's just biding his time until when?" a stern voice in the back of her mind demanded.

The timing would be right if Monica had been just beginning the pregnancy when Joe left for Arabia. Kate hadn't met her then; there was no way for her to know the facts. But the date of their births certainly worked out in favor of the idea. Then why had Joe not just told her he thought he might be their father—maybe even knew for a fact that he was? Monica could have suspected and told Joe, and he'd just opted to go on with his assignment and left her to fend for herself and the baby. But if he had a change of heart after all this time, wouldn't he have come storming into their lives demanding his rights to his children?

Whereas, I have no rights. The realization struck her with such impact, she moaned aloud. Fortunately, the others were making so much noise themselves they didn't hear her. She turned away and groped for a tissue in her bag, blotting at tears that had spurted instantly. No, she wouldn't have it! The children were hers; she'd earned the right to call herself their mother, and nobody was going to take that away from her. She blew her nose and turned back.

The three of them had moved up along the fence and were calling out to a large, recumbent gorilla who had no intention of allowing the silly humans to interrupt his nap.

"Mommy, come and see," Robbie called out.

Kate waved and smiled. Joe grinned and gestured toward the hot dog vendor at the end of the block. She nodded, keeping her smile grimly in place.

"Go ahead," she called out, "I'll catch up."

She watched the three of them stroll away, hand in hand. Why would Joe be hanging around, pretending to be their friend, pretending to be investigating Monica's death, if his real motivation was only to claim paternity?

He wouldn't.

And of course, Wilkins's death was real, so the possible threat to their lives was real. That made the chances good that Joe was exactly whom he claimed to be and his motives were all up front and aboveboard.

She inhaled a deep sigh of relief. "One of these days you ought to put that imagination to work writing spy novels, Kate my girl," she muttered.

She yelled after the others and then ran to catch up with them.

She was going to spend the rest of the day enjoying the outing, concentrating on giving the twins as fine a time as possible, and tonight she and Joe were going to get into the brownstone and into the apartment. They'd find the key and solve the mystery. Her mind couldn't contrive the details of how the key would change anything, or how it would end the threat to her, but optimism was the flavor of the day, as of this moment. And then Joe Riley would be on his way back to his own life, she and the twins would remember him fondly as they got on with their own...*and someday her prince would come.*

She was laughing to herself as she caught up with her family.

KATE RANG THE BELL of apartment 2A and waited, trying not to turn around and look pointedly at Joe, who was standing in one of the shop entrances across the street. The murky street lamps were spaced far enough apart to allow full darkness in the recessed doorways.

No answer. Her hand was shaking as she reached up and pushed the bell again. Still no answer. She was about to gesture to Joe to come over when the door opened behind her and two people came out of the building.

"Oh, it's really nice out," the woman said. "Let's walk."

They passed Kate without appearing to notice her and went down the steps.

Kate took a deep breath and turned back to the board, keeping her face averted in case one of them looked back.

She watched the couple stroll up the street, and when they reached the far corner, she gestured to Joe.

He dashed across the street, not even bothering to look out for traffic, and Kate gasped as a car swerved to avoid hitting him.

"Are you trying to get killed before we do this?" she snapped as he came panting up beside her.

"I still think we should use the back entry," Joe muttered, ignoring her censure.

"And get caught by Santos?"

"So how do we get in?"

"It's an old New York trick." She rang the bell for apartment 3B. The intercom crackled and an irritated voice demanded to know who was there.

Kate pressed the response button. "I've got a package here for 1B—nobody's home. Can you come down and get it?"

A snort of derision crackled over the intercom. "Yeah, right! Forget it, lady!"

"Well, if you won't come down, can you buzz me

into the foyer so I can leave it by the mailboxes, please?''

There was a static-filled moment of delay and Kate held her hand up, fingers crossed.

They both jumped as the buzzer sounded raucously behind them. Joe grabbed the doorknob and twisted. The door opened and they rushed inside.

''Lucky,'' Joe whispered.

''Not luck,'' Kate refuted, ''common sense. Most people aren't going to go down three flights of stairs to get someone else's package. The alternatives? Either ignore me or buzz me in and forgo all further responsibility.''

And it probably didn't hurt that the messenger was a woman, Joe thought.

Kate led the way up the staircase, a cautioning hand on Joe's arm. Stopping for a moment, she tilted her head and listened for sounds of footsteps in the halls. Hearing none, she continued upward, Joe keeping step beside her.

They turned left at the top of the landing and moved on stealthy feet toward the apartment on the right.

''Wait,'' Joe ordered as Kate was about to insert the master key into the lock. He leaned around her and pressed the bell on the doorjamb.

''What are you doing?'' Kate hissed.

Joe put his finger to his lips. He leaned forward and whispered against her ear. ''What if the tenant was just in the shower when you rang downstairs, or sleeping? Just making sure it's safe.''

Kate nodded, panic welling up to suffocate her as she realized she might well have led them into a very nasty situation.

Joe saw her dismay and rubbed her shoulder. "It's okay," he whispered, "I don't think anyone's home."

Kate's hands were useless. After a futile, fumbled attempt, she turned and handed the key to Joe.

"Don't turn the lights on," she warned from behind him as they entered the darkened apartment. "The apartment faces the street."

Joe nodded and put his arm around her to shut the door. The sound of the latch clicking into place was like a gunshot in the quiet, making Kate jerk with alarm.

"Can you remember your way around in the dark?" Joe asked at her ear.

Kate nodded. "I think so. It's not all that big. The bedrooms are straight ahead down the hall, living room to our left and kitchen beyond that."

She turned her head and saw that there was a dim light coming from the street into the living room through uncurtained windows. The long, narrow hall would be the darkest space of all, and she faced it with trepidation.

"Okay, you lead the way to Monica's old room, and I'll hang on to you."

His hand on her arm steadied her as much as it helped guide him forward. She moved cautiously, aware that the tenant might have things lying in the hall that would trip them up.

She stopped abruptly and Joe muttered as he stumbled up against her. "What's the matter?" he hissed.

She could feel the sibilance against her ear. For a moment she knew a terrible urge to turn and fall into his arms, clinging for dear life.

"I'm trying to get used to the dark, and to make sure I don't trip on anything," she whispered weakly.

Joe ran his hand up her back and squeezed her shoulder. "Smart move, babe."

Kate took a deep breath and shuffled her feet forward, finding only bare wood floor in front of her. In this fashion they moved down the long hall to the back bedroom Monica had shared with the twins.

Relief almost caused Kate to cry aloud when she opened the door and saw that the light from a room in the brownstone next door cast enough of a glow to alleviate the darkness. She could make out a king-size bed and the furniture that lined the walls. The closet door was a white rectangle that beckoned and quickened her step.

She could smell the faint aftershave or cologne the tenant favored as she moved clothing on hangers to fit her hand under the shelf. For a moment the sweetness of it overwhelmed her and she stepped back.

"Are you okay?"

Kate swallowed. It was just nerves. Get a grip, she told herself, and moved back in place, reaching up to the shelf.

"It's here," she gasped, only that moment realizing that she'd never dared hope they'd actually find it.

Her fingers worked at the tape that covered the key, but she couldn't get an edge loosened.

"Here, let me," Joe whispered, easing in beside her. After a moment she heard his sigh of relief. "Got it," he muttered, his tone triumphant.

He turned and pushed her gently forward. "Let's get out of here," he said, "and let's leave the door open. It might help us see better in the hall."

They were at the door, ready to leave the apartment, when they heard voices on the other side.

Without a word they rushed back down the hall, unmindful of any obstacles that might trip them up. Joe was behind Kate; when they reached the back bedroom and he heard the front door open, he shoved Kate ahead of him into the closet.

Just as Joe was pulling the closet door toward him, they heard a male voice call out, "I'll just be a minute. My jacket's in the closet."

Kate's knees gave way and she slipped down to the floor, her heart pounding so hard she was sure the tenant would hear it the minute he entered the room. Joe pushed to the back of the closet, trying to get behind the hanging clothes without clunking hangers against the rod.

The fragrance that had bothered her before was suffocating now, and she feared she was going to sneeze, or worse, to gag. She clamped her hand over her mouth and squeezed her eyes shut, one arm wrapped around her waist as she curled into a fetal ball. *My poor babies! How will they ever live down the shame of their mother being in prison?*

The hand on her shoulder caused her to jerk upright and she heard the hangers clang together as Joe stumbled back.

Joe's hand. Kate shivered and huddled further into herself.

They both stopped breathing, waiting for the door to be wrenched open, to face discovery.

The silence seemed to stretch on forever.

Sweat poured down on Joe's face and crept beneath the collar of his shirt, making his skin itch. He didn't dare move.

Kate thought the trembling in all her limbs was the onset of permanent paralysis. Her teeth felt frozen in their fierce grip, and the tears in her eyes would have blinded her if she'd been able to see in the darkness of the closet in the first place.

Joe's head shot up when he heard the front door open and then slam shut. His breath escaped his chest in a whoosh and he slumped back against the wall, gasping aloud. It seemed to take him a moment to gather his senses.

"They're gone," he whispered, leaning toward Kate. "It must have been in another closet."

She didn't respond. Didn't move.

"Kate, come on, we've got to get out of here!"

Nothing.

He slammed open the door and knelt beside her. "Kate! Katie, are you all right?"

Kate felt the draft of cooler air wash over her, felt Joe's hands moving over her arms, shoulders and back. Maybe she wasn't paralyzed, after all.

She gingerly lifted her head. "Joe?"

"It's all right, honey, they're gone. We're safe."

She threw herself into his arms in a torrent of tears, babbling about what would become of her children when she went to jail.

Joe tried not to laugh, tried not to enjoy the feel of her in his arms, clinging to him. "We've got to go," he said against her head.

She nodded but still she clung to him, sobbing and shaking.

"Kate, do you need me to carry you?"

The suggestion seemed to penetrate. Taking great gulping breaths and scrubbing her face with her fists, Kate managed to pull herself together. She grabbed the sleeve of one of the shirts hanging beside her and wiped her eyes with it.

Joe eased her out of the closet.

They were at the door of the bedroom when Kate pulled out of his grasp and dug in her heels.

"What's the matter now?"

"I'm not taking any chances. I'm not going out that front door."

"Is there a back door?"

"No." A stray sob hiccupped behind the word.

"Then how else can we get out of here?"

"The fire escape." She went to the window and pulled it up.

"Kate, honey, that isn't necessary. If we're careful, I'm sure…"

"I'm not going out the front door."

Joe could see Kate wasn't going to yield. It reminded him of Ashleigh's doggedness when she'd made up her mind.

"Lead on, Macduff," he said, grinning and bowing toward the open window.

The fire escape led down to the alley beside the brownstone, and they had a brief scare when they saw that Mr. Santos's window was wide open, but they crept by without incident.

They entered the first brightly lit coffee shop they came to and sat grinning tremulously at each other, relief palpable between them, until the waitress came to take their order. It was only after they'd had the first restorative cup of coffee that Joe took the key out of his pocket and set it on the table.

They stared at it in mute wonder.

Kate broke the silence as she reached out and caressed the outline of the key with one finger. "Are you sure there weren't instructions taped up there with it?"

Joe kept his expression solemn. "I didn't look. I guess there's nothing to do but go back and find out."

When he saw the way her complexion paled, the look of absolute horror on her face, he was instantly chastened.

"My God, Kate," he whispered, "I was just kidding."

Kate glared at him. "Get over yourself, Riley. You didn't fool me for a minute."

But she gulped a second cup of coffee without feeling the heat and wished to hell she'd never given up smoking.

"There's nothing about it to indicate what it might unlock," Joe said, turning the key every which way. "It's not a car key, not a locker key, not a safety deposit box key." He scratched his head and grimaced. "Now we know what it ain't—all we have to do is figure out what it *is*."

Kate couldn't find any humor in the situation. "We just committed a crime, risked our necks for nothing," she said, slapping her palm on the tabletop for emphasis.

Joe flinched. "You don't know it's for nothing. We've just begun our investigation. We may stumble across some helpful clues yet."

Suddenly it all seemed too much to Kate. The whole business of running, hiding, breaking the law, looking for straws. And for what? There wasn't any proof someone was after them. Nothing but Joe Riley's word. Wilkins's death didn't even have to support Joe's theory; his murder could easily have no connection to Kate or Monica whatsoever.

"*Stumble* is the operative word here, Riley," Kate said, standing up and slinging her bag over her shoulder. "I say we forget the whole damned thing, go back and get the kids and go home."

Joe had to let the waitress keep the change from the ten, the smallest bill he had, in order to get out of the café quickly enough to catch up with Kate before she could flag down a cab.

They rode back to the hotel in silence.

Donna had the children bathed and in pajamas, but had given in to their pleas to stay up and watch a favorite Disney film.

Kate quickly nipped their little drama in the bud as she turned off the TV and marched them off to bed.

Joe assured Donna that Kate wasn't angry with her and insisted on walking her down and directing her to the care of the doorman, who would see her safely into a cab. He stopped to chat with the clerk at the tobacco counter, bought a paper, exchanged a few remarks about the weather with one of the desk clerks.

When he returned to the suite, the other bedroom door was closed and only one lamp remained lit in the living room. He stood outside the bedroom door and listened. Obviously Kate had gone to bed.

Just as well, he thought, going to his own room. She'd get over her miff in the morning, and they'd be able to come to an agreement about what their next move should be.

But what if, he wondered as he brushed his teeth, she really meant it about going back home? Could he protect her if whoever was after her found her there? And what about when it was time to report back on his job? Who would look after her then?

He dropped his shirt and jeans in the laundry bag that hung on the hook on the bathroom door and went into the bedroom.

As he closed his eyes and prepared for sleep, he told himself again that Kate would come around by morning. Somehow it ended up being more like a prayer than a fact.

IN HER ROOM KATE HUNG UP the phone. The conversation she'd just had with Terri Maynard left her with mixed feelings. If someone had disappeared from her life, without explanation, without making contact for almost six years, would she have been as effusive as Terri had been? She didn't think so. She plumped her pillow and lay down. Funny, she didn't remember Terri as the bubbly, perky type at all, but just now, on the phone, Terri had gushed and squealed excitedly at hearing from Kate.

In contrast to that, Terri hadn't even seemed interested in where Kate had been all this time, had never asked why she left. She had asked where Kate was now, where she was staying, how long she'd be in the city. She'd just kept insisting over and over that they had to get together, meet for a meal, a drink, whatever.

A regular homecoming party, Kate thought, turning on her side.

"Why am I feeling so suspicious?" Kate whispered into her pillow. It was that damned Joe Riley. He'd turned her into a paranoid wimp, looking for danger at every turn. Well, she'd had enough of that. She'd taken care of herself—and the kids—in the past; she'd do it again. Joe Riley might think he was all that, but he was in for a surprise come morning.

Chapter Ten

"Here's what we're going to do," Kate said as she closed the door behind Donna and the children. "We're going to take the key to Skinner at the Kismet Club." She leaned her head against the door, keeping her back to Joe.

Joe jumped up from the breakfast table. "What?" He stalked over to her and grasped her arm to turn her toward him. "Why?"

"Monica worked at the club. She was found in the alley behind the club. She had a relationship with Skinner. Whatever the key unlocks, Skinner is the one person most likely to know what Monica was about."

Joe studied her face. Clearly she'd given this a lot of thought. And he couldn't find fault with her theory. He nodded.

"All right. I'll call and ask for an appointment to see him."

"No." Kate pulled him back. "The more off guard he is, the better chance we have of learning something. If he's expecting us, he'll have time to put a leash on his true emotions, to contrive a story."

Joe grinned and said softly, "The sleeping beast awakens."

She returned his smile, her own quizzical. "Did you think I was one of those meek, submissive women who could only move if I had a man to lead me?"

He raised his hand and ran the back of his fingers along her jaw. "Could anyone know Ashleigh and believe that of her mother? For that matter, could anyone know the details of the way you made a life for yourself and those kids and believe that?"

Kate swallowed with difficulty, moved as much by his comment as by his gentle caress. She could smell the faint scent of his aftershave on his fingers, the fragrance calling to places within her that hadn't been aroused in a long while.

Her eyes were large and round, beseeching, as she gazed up into his face. "Don't misunderstand our... connection, Joe. This is a temporary situation."

Joe stepped back, feeling as if she'd slapped him. He could no longer resist this feeling of intimacy developing between them. But was it only his own feeling? No, she must have recognized it to be rejecting it now. If she felt it as well, he had only to step forward, take her into his arms and close the gap.

But she'd rejected his advance before he'd even thought to make it. And Joe was nothing if not a gentleman. His jaw tightened and he turned away. Kate would have to make the first move, pose an invitation, before he touched her again. The thought that it might never happen left him feeling bereft, but this wasn't the time to examine that.

"I'll get my jacket," he said.

Kate watched him walk toward his room, and she clutched her fist to her stomach. So close, she thought. Just a breath of movement and she could have been in his arms, could have known the pleasure of cleaving to him, to his warmth, his strength, his riveting masculinity. She could feel herself surrounded by that delicious fragrance, her body electrified by his touch.

A blink of sanity penetrated her mind. *And suffer the consequences when he's gone, leaving you alone and unfit for any other man,* the little voice whispered.

Thank goodness she'd had the sense to call a halt before that moment, she congratulated herself. But the hollow feeling in her stomach persisted as she hurried to her room to get ready.

She was just applying a light brush of mascara to her lashes when she heard a movement in the doorway.

"Kate, do you have the car keys? I can't find them."

Kate swore under her breath and reached for a tissue to blot the black smear on her cheek. "I don't know, Joe," she snapped, "look in my backpack."

He returned a moment later, jiggling the keys. "Found them. Are these your parents?"

His question made no sense. She looked up and saw he was holding something in his hands. It was the framed photo.

"Where did you find that?" she asked, his image behind her in the mirror.

"It was in your backpack." He carried it into the room and set it on the desk in front of her. "Nice-looking family. Your college graduation?"

Kate nodded, looking down at the picture.

"Yes."

She could see him recalling what she'd told him that night in the motel. "You never saw them again," he said softly.

Their eyes met in the mirror, his radiating sorrow for her.

She shook her head. "No." She reached out and traced a finger over the glass, outlining her mother's image. It still hurt to know they were no longer in the world with her, that she could never reach out to them, hear their voices, feel their hugs, see their smiles of pride and love.

She thought of her own children. If it was hard to lose your parents in your twenties, what would it feel like if you were six years old?

"We'd better go," she said abruptly. She grabbed her bag off the desk, shoved the picture inside and moved around Joe to get her jacket out of the closet.

"We aren't driving, are we?" she asked, looking pointedly at the keys in Joe's hand.

"No. I just noticed I didn't have them and I was concerned that I might have lost them."

He followed her out to the hall, turning to check that the door locked itself when he'd pulled it closed.

"Do you want to walk?" he asked over his shoulder.

Kate tilted her head, considering the location of the Kismet in relation to the hotel. "I guess. If it isn't too windy."

They emerged from the lobby into a typical day, though the clouds had a gray tinge to them and there was a strong breeze. Still, it wasn't too cool to walk and they fell in step, side by side, Joe with his hands in his jacket pockets, Kate with one hand on the strap of her shoulder bag, the other clasped over it.

Joe glanced sidewise at her, recalling her easy stride, her bag swinging free on her back, when he'd followed her in Lake George. "The old habits return in a hurry," he said, nodding his head at her grim grip on her purse.

She shrugged. "No sense looking for trouble," she said. But wasn't she doing just that, her mind urged.

Going to brave the lion in his den, as it were. Automatically seeking comfort, she took her left hand off her bag and slipped it under Joe's arm.

The Kismet was a walk-down in a brownstone building with a discreet neon sign at street level. To Kate it looked the same as it had the time she'd been there more than five years ago. She remembered a squeamish feeling then and experienced it now. She remembered the interior had been dark, gloomy, that she'd felt uneasy in the presence of the sinister faces she'd seen peering out of the haze of smoke that hung over the tables. Monica had teased that Kate was just unfamiliar with the nightclub scene, but the feelings hadn't let up then or even when they'd returned home after Monica had finished her sets. She'd suggested often after that, that Monica get an agent and start singing in other clubs. Of course Monica hadn't taken her advice, and she'd been murdered a few months later.

A chill ran up Kate's spine as they started down the stairs.

Joe felt the tremor in Kate's hand and halted. "Would you rather not do this, Kate?"

Kate raised her chin and took a deep breath of the fresh air as if to create a reserve in her lungs before entering the stale miasma she was sure awaited them inside.

"I'm fine," she said, smiling brightly.

Either they'd improved the ventilation system since her last visit, or the fact that there were only a few patrons there in the daytime hours made the interior less stifling. There was even natural light in the main room, coming in from the street-level windows set above the bar. True, there was a stream of smoke from the two drinkers with cigarettes in their hands, caught in the shaft of sunlight that spilled through the windows, but it didn't clutch at her chest, make it difficult to breathe.

Joe led the way to the bar and they climbed onto stools and awaited the bartender, who'd barely acknowledged their arrival.

He made his idle way toward them, swiping at the bar top with a damp cloth en route.

"'Do for you, folks?" he asked.

"Mr. Springer in?" Joe pushed an ashtray out of the way and put his elbows on the bar.

Kate studied the bartender's face and decided she hadn't seen him before.

The man returned her gaze and then looked Joe over. He nodded and reached for a phone behind the bar.

"Something to drink while you wait?" he suggested.

"No, thanks," Kate replied, speaking for both of them. She couldn't imagine unclenching her teeth to put a glass to her mouth, let alone swallowing past the lump in her throat.

They wouldn't have had time for a drink, in any case. Only moments later a large, burly, bejowled man came up behind them. "Follow me" was all he said, but it was clearly an order. When they turned on the bar stools, they could see that he was wearing a holster containing a gun.

He led them to a small elevator off a tiny hall beyond the main room. It was a claustrophobic fit, given the man's size and his harsh, labored breathing. The elevator labored as well, creaking and groaning as it made its tortuous way up to the third floor. By the time the gate unfolded, Kate was ready to exchange the smoke-filled Saturday night air of any club in the city for that in the elevator.

There were two doors in the hall, one facing them and one at the far end on their right. The man approached the one directly opposite the elevator and rapped once on the frosted glass of the window insert.

The office they entered was not the plush quarters of a man who pampered himself in his workplace, though it was a fairly large room. There were beige metal file cabinets lining the wall behind the old, scarred wooden desk, two wooden chairs along the wall next to the door they'd entered. The cabinets ended at another door, now closed, which Kate thought might lead to a closet or a bathroom. The only sign of opulence was a matching pair of tapestried wing chairs facing the desk. As if Springer catered to the comfort of guests though he denied himself.

She'd remembered him as menacing, but the man seated behind the desk had a serious, businesslike appearance that didn't match her memory. He didn't look like the kind of man who employed thugs for bodyguards, though it was clear their escort was just that.

The bodyguard took a seat on a wooden chair near the door as Don Springer motioned the two of them to the impressive upholstered chairs in front of his desk.

"Don't I know you?" He addressed Kate as she moved to one of the chairs.

Kate cleared her throat. "I'm Katelynn Adams. I was a friend of Monica's—her roommate, in fact."

Springer studied her face a moment longer and nodded before turning his attention to Joe. "And you?"

"We've never met. But I knew Monica as well." He offered his hand. "Joe Riley."

They shook. Everyone sat down.

All very congenial and polite, Kate thought, staring

at the man behind the desk, as though we weren't here to discuss murder and perhaps other crimes.

Springer spoke first.

"Monica's been dead for over five years. If this concerns her death, you've taken your time about coming to see me."

"Does that mean you know something, knew something back then?" Kate demanded.

Springer's smile was slow. Without turning his head, he spoke in a low tone. "Manny, we have a lot of reservations for tonight. Jake's going to need help stocking the bar."

He waited until the bodyguard had left the room.

"How well did you know Monica, Ms. Adams?"

"We lived together for six months before she died. I was her children's baby-sitter as well as her friend."

Springer seemed to fold in upon himself, his erect stature crumpling before their eyes.

When he began to speak, Kate had to lean forward to hear him clearly.

"I'd have given anything to protect Monica. I tried to warn her...she was...headstrong...greedy...she..." His voice trailed away and he took out a handkerchief and wiped his mouth.

His eyes were bleak when he raised his head. "The children...you know what happened to them?"

Joe gasped, but neither Springer nor Kate seemed to notice. Did Springer think the twins were his? Had Monica told him they were? No! Impossible!

"What's your interest in Monica's children?" Joe demanded, his voice harsh, his face etched with suspicion.

Springer looked at Joe, his own expression registering surprise. "Only that they were hers. I...I loved her, you know. I knew what she was but...I loved her."

Kate felt herself softening. Was she wrong about Skinner? Was it possible he wasn't the sleaze she'd always suspected? Could his feelings for Monica have been real? And what about Monica, herself? Could Kate have been so unaware of her friend's shortcomings? Skinner had called her greedy but in Kate's view, Monica had been generous to a fault. Still, there were all kinds of greed....

"The children are with me," she admitted impulsively, "and have been all along. As Monica requested."

It was as if a light came on behind Skinner's blue eyes.

"I wonder...did Monica give you a...an *item,* to hold for her, as well?"

He seemed to be leaning into the question, his body pushed forward over the desktop, his eyes piercing.

In point of fact, the key certainly qualified as an "item." She glanced at Joe and saw the warning in his eyes, the slight shake of his head.

"I'm not sure I understand what you're asking," Kate said, stalling, waiting to see where Joe was going with this. After all, they'd agreed to give the key to Skinner, to enlist his help in finding out what it was for.

Joe leaned forward himself. "If you want to know anything about a missing *item,*" he said, emphasizing the word as Skinner had, "you're going to have to answer some of our questions first."

Skinner turned his attention to Joe with a raised eyebrow and a bristling tone.

"What have you got to do with all this, Riley?"

"Ms. Adams and I are partners. You might say I'm here to protect her interests. And as I think I mentioned, Monica and I were friends."

Joe could appear pretty menacing himself. His whole appearance seemed to grow larger as he focused on Skinner.

"I think you know exactly what happened to Monica and why. Or maybe you killed her yourself!"

Skinner's reaction to Joe's accusation was immediate and unexpected. Once again he seemed to collapse, and for a moment Kate feared the man was on the verge of heart failure.

"If you know so much, you know the cops fingered the shooter," he protested, but his voice was weak.

"And figured him for a hit man," Joe snapped. "You may not have pulled the trigger, but that doesn't mean…"

"No!" Skinner all but screamed the denial as he jumped out of his chair.

Joe didn't react. Calmly he said, "But you know who did."

Skinner hesitated. Kate could almost see the wheels spinning in his mind. Suddenly he slumped back in his seat and nodded his head, his hands turned upward as if in supplication.

"What's the difference? You won't be able to use anything I tell you. There's no proof. And it looks like Monica took the package to the grave with her."

"Package? What package?" Kate asked.

Skinner studied her face, as if trying to see into her mind, trying to test her innocence. Apparently satisfied with what he saw there, he shrugged and began to speak.

"I was in business for myself back then. At least on

paper.'' He wiped his brow and sighed. ''But I had associates, who expected certain…uh…favors….''

He turned away from the couple, looking out of the window beside his desk. It seemed to help him focus on the past.

''Periodically they'd put a certain amount of money into my protective custody, as it were, and I'd start it on its way through…channels.''

''Money laundering,'' Joe said.

Skinner ignored him and went on.

''They brought one of those packages a few nights before Monica…'' He stopped and gestured over his shoulder. ''My living quarters are right next door.'' Both Joe and Kate followed his gesture at the second door in the room.

''Monica was in there that night. We'd just…she was getting dressed when Manny rang up to tell me my associates were on their way up to the office. I told Monica to let herself out by the hall door and I left the apartment.''

He cleared his throat. ''I never gave her another thought. I figured she'd left only seconds after I came in here.

''They were only in here a couple of minutes, long enough to give me their usual instructions. I opened the safe—'' he pointed to the wall behind them ''—just as they were leaving. As I approached the desk to get the package, the alarm buzzer went off—it's a signal from downstairs that there's trouble in the back room.''

Kate interrupted. ''The back room?''

Springer nodded. ''A gaming room at the back of the club downstairs.'' He looked down at his hands folded on the desktop.

"It could have been a raid…anything…I just rushed out without a thought. The door locks automatically…I guess if I was thinking at all, I figured I'd be gone only minutes, that the package was safe up here…." He shook his head and pounded his clasped fists on the desk. "I never figured Monica was still up here, would come into the office…."

Joe leaned forward, his voice low. "Monica took the money?"

Springer raised his head and smiled grimly.

"When I got back up here, my mind was still caught up in the business downstairs. The safe was closed. I thought I'd already transferred the package and closed the safe before running out. I figured it was automatic on my part and that the emergency downstairs had blocked it out of my mind."

His hands trembled as he lifted them to his face. "I went back to the apartment and of course Monica was gone. I went back downstairs and spent the rest of the night taking care of things in the club. I never checked the safe until morning."

"You suspected Monica right away?" Joe asked.

Kate had been thinking about that. Skinner said he loved Monica. So given that, would she have been the first person he'd point the finger at? If the door between the apartment and the office wasn't on automatic lock, as Skinner had said the door to the hall was, couldn't just about anyone have got in that way, seen the package, taken off with it? Any and all of his employees could have known he lived up here and that there was a door right from the apartment into the office.

As if reading her thoughts, Skinner shook his head.

"Monica was the last person I thought of, to tell you the truth. Oh, I knew she liked nice things, was always after me for gifts, money…I just never figured her for stealing from me.

"But then Monica didn't show up for her first set the next night. I called her apartment and there was no answer." He stared at Kate.

Kate tried to recall the nights leading up to the night Monica was killed. Had she gone out somewhere? If she had, the twins would have been with Mrs. Jackson, the alternate sitter who lived across the street in an apartment up over the dry cleaner's. She shrugged. "I can't remember anything of that week before that night," she admitted, frowning at Skinner.

Skinner shrugged. "She didn't come in for the second set, either. Meanwhile the associates were all over me, demanding answers, threatening me. We'd questioned all the employees and nobody else could be figured for the deed. When she didn't come in the next night, it began to look suspicious. I called the apartment again and you told me she had already left for work."

Kate couldn't recall the conversation. But that wasn't surprising; it would have seemed like a run-of-the-mill call if Springer hadn't conveyed any urgency by tone or word.

And where was Monica on those two nights that she'd left the apartment ostensibly to go to the club? She thought about the cash in the video case. It had seemed a large amount to have at hand in the apartment, even given its ingenious hiding place, but not large enough to add up to mob money. Could she have been out stashing it somewhere? Somewhere, someplace, that the key would unlock?

Springer went on, interrupting her thoughts. "The m—associates…got suspicious when she didn't go on for her usual sets. They knew we had a thing going, knew she spent a lot of time up in my apartment. They gave me a couple of hours to locate her, get her in here for questioning.''

''How did she happen to be here the night she was killed?'' Kate asked. ''Out in the alley, anyway?''

Springer stood abruptly and went over to the window where he leaned against the jamb, his arms folded across his chest, his face in profile to them.

''She came in to work as if nothing had happened. I was so relieved to see her I almost wept. Look, I asked the guys when they phoned, would she be here if she'd taken the package? Not likely. I laughed it off, said she was a prima donna, took advantage of our relationship to come and go as she pleased. They didn't buy it. They said they were going to come in to talk to her. They got here while she was doing her next-to-last number of the first set. We were arguing about it at the bar. I could see Monica up on the stand, watching us as she sang. When she finished the set she went right back to where the dressing rooms are. There's a back door that leads right out to the alley.''

He turned to them, his eyes bleak. ''When she didn't come back into the bar as she usually did, the guys went looking for her.'' He sighed.

''I never saw her again.''

Kate's muffled sob reverberated in the room. Joe reached over and caught her hand, holding it tightly in his own.

''They didn't find the money and yet they let you off the hook?'' Joe asked the other man, his voice deepened by disbelief.

Springer's laugh was a bleat of despair. ''I was lucky they didn't kill me as well. The mob has a way of

settling their own terms of justice. They figured the
worth of the club, the building as well as the business,
was equal to what I'd lost of their money, with maybe
a little extra thrown in for penalty costs. I signed the
deeds over in exchange for my life. As a final act of
contrition, they expected me to stay on, at a salary, and
continue to manage the place.''

He returned to his desk. ''That's it. That's everything.''

''Not quite,'' Joe said, rising now himself. ''What
about Wilkins?''

Kate was watching Springer's face. He couldn't have
been more bewildered. ''Wilkins? Who's he?''

''Matt Wilkins. The private detective I hired to in-
vestigate. He came here to talk to your people when
you were out of town. Told me he was coming back
to see you.''

Springer looked thoughtful and then opened a
drawer at the side of his desk. He lifted out a box and
opened it to reveal a mess of cards. Matt Wilkins's was
near the top. He pulled it out, looked at it a moment
and then nodded. ''Yeah, I forgot his name. Yeah, he
was one of the guys came asking questions. I didn't
have anything for him. I sure as hell wasn't going to
tell him what I just told you. P.I.'s are almost as bad
as cops when it comes to stirring up a can of worms.
I don't need that. I sent him on his way. End of that
story.''

''It certainly was,'' Joe said, his expression grim.
''He was killed after he saw you.''

Springer sat down. He had to crane his neck to look
up at Joe, who still hovered over the desk. He shook
his head. ''No way. You're way off track here if you
think it has anything to do with me.''

"What about your associates?" Joe asked, putting a sarcastic spin on the euphemism Springer kept using.

"The people who did Monica didn't even know Wilkins existed. Why would I mention it to them? My debt to them was long paid. I wasn't going to start them thinking about the past, that's for damned sure."

"What about me?" Kate said. "If the mob was satisfied with the deal they made with you for the club, why are they still coming after me?"

Springer blinked. And blinked again. And then he chuckled softly. "Believe me, Ms. Adams, you were never in it after that. Once they checked out the apartment and didn't find the money, they came straight back here where the man was baby-sitting me to make sure I didn't try to run. The deal was made that night. I'd bet my life they never even knew your name, never thought to go looking for you."

The look of shock on both their faces wiped the smile off Springer's own.

"You still don't get it?" He spoke as though they were children to whom he was explaining a complicated concept.

"The mob has a long memory if they think they've been ripped off. But they have their own convoluted sense of justice. Once they consider a bill paid, in whatever currency they choose, the matter is over. Case closed.

"I can assure you, Ms. Adams, if someone is after you, it isn't the mob."

Chapter Eleven

It took a moment for Kate to absorb what Springer was saying. With enlightenment came dread. She turned her head slowly and stared at Joe Riley.

Of course. Had she ever been threatened directly by anyone? No! She had not been approached by anyone but Riley. Could he have used the threat of danger to her and the children to entice her to run off with him? *The threat Springer had emphatically insisted didn't exist!* But why?

What could Riley have to gain by such manipulation, by an involvement with them? She felt the knot of dread grow to a full-size lump in her throat as she realized how gullible she'd been, how easily she'd fallen in with his machinations.

Humiliation became anger, starting as a hum and growing to a roar in her mind. She almost missed Springer's next words.

"Listen, if you did find something…well, technically it's mine. I don't think my associates would take a trade-off—this property has turned out to be far more valuable to them—but it would be some compensation for me."

The money. Of course. That's what Riley was after.

As was Springer. For all his protestations of love for Monica, the bottom line was still about money.

She stood up, her body rigid with cold contempt, and slammed the key on the desktop.

"What's this?"

Her smile was feral. "I don't know. It's what Monica left behind. You two can fight over it or work together to figure it out. I don't give a damn! Personally, I don't think it has anything to do with your filthy money—I don't believe for a minute that Monica stole anything. So as far as I can see, my best friend, my children's mother, died for nothing!"

Before the two men could react, she ran out of the office and, ignoring the elevator, made for the stairs.

Joe came tearing out of the building just minutes behind Kate, just in time to see her dash out into the street.

It had begun to rain while they were inside, a steady downpour that darkened the sky and put a patent-leather sheen on the streets. Kate's hair was already plastered to her head, her clothes hanging limply from dampness.

All the sights and sounds, all movement, suddenly turned to slow motion as he watched a car come speeding down the street, aimed directly at Kate. He watched, his heart in his mouth, his mouth open in a silent scream, as Kate's head turned, causing her hair to fly out behind her, a red banner that formed a perfect target for the oncoming car.

For a moment it was as if time and space were caught in a frame where all sound, all movement, was frozen, and he was deaf, dumb and paralyzed.

Sensation returned in a cacophony of sounds that

pummeled him from all sides as he dashed into the street to fall beside Kate's prone body.

The car had missed her by mere inches, and only because in that last desperate moment she'd had the presence of mind to leap out of its relentless path.

Joe was running his hands over her limbs and back, repeating her name over and over, begging her to talk to him, mindless of the rain that fell on his face, streamed down the collar of his shirt.

"You're making a fool of yourself, Riley," she groaned as she pushed herself to a sitting position and swatted his hands away.

"Leave me alone," she snapped. "I'm not hurt and nothing is broken."

Someone loomed over her and she looked up. Springer. He, at least, had had the presence of mind to grab an umbrella; it shadowed his face, giving it the menacing quality she'd always imagined there.

He frowned and exchanged a look with Joe.

"Looks like your girlfriend's made some powerful enemies, Riley."

Joe got to his feet, his hands fisted, ready to do battle.

Springer raised the hand that wasn't clasping the umbrella, palm out, and shook his head. "I'm not one of them, pal, I assure you."

"Should we call an ambulance, mister?" a young woman asked.

"Yes, please," Joe said.

"No!" Ignoring her aching bones, Kate jumped to her feet. "I'm fine. No ambulance."

Ignoring Joe, she hailed the cab that was idling at the curb across the street.

"Where are you going, Kate?" Joe grabbed her arm as she started to get into the back of the taxi.

"Back to the hotel to get my kids," she said, and pulled away.

"Fine. Good idea." He got in and pushed her over before she could protest.

The driver looked over his shoulder. "That was a close call you had, lady. That guy looked determined as hell to run you down."

"You saw the guy?" Joe asked, leaning forward.

"Saw the car," the cabbie corrected him.

"Did you get the license?"

"Naw, happened too fast, and the rain and all. But it was an Audi, I'm pretty sure."

Kate sat in the corner, arms folded over her waist, trying not to admit to herself that her insides were suddenly quaking.

"You okay?" Joe asked, turning to her.

She stared at him, wanting to scream her fury. *What do you want? Why are you here? Who are you?*

Instead, she nodded, and then looked away from his beseeching glance to stare out of the window.

The silence between them was broken only by the rhythmical swishing of the windshield wipers.

It wasn't until she tried to get out of the cab that she felt the toil of delayed reaction on her body. That, added to the bruised feeling all over, caused her legs to buckle as she tried to put her weight on them to stand. Her damp body was chilled, her teeth chattering with it. Joe shoved some money at the cabbie and scooted over to catch her just as she started to fall back into the seat.

The doorman rushed forward and helped her out, holding her steady until Joe slid over and came out beside her, holding an umbrella over her despite the fact that it was too late to keep her dry.

Joe kept a grip on her arm as they made their silent ascent in the elevator, and all the way down the hall to their suite.

The warmth of the suite caressed her skin, only then making her aware of the chill that invaded every pore. She began to shake, clenching her teeth and her fists, doubling over as tears spilled from her eyes.

"We don't want the kids to see you like this," Joe said.

He picked her up as easily as if she were one of the twins and cradled her to his chest.

"Shock," he whispered. "It'll pass." He said more, but his words were unintelligible to her, as if he were speaking in tongues.

He carried her into his bedroom and shut the door with his foot. Going to the chair, he sat with her on his lap, rocking back and forth, holding her as if she were a fragile treasure, steadily speaking in a low drone.

She became aware of fragmented sentences.

"...didn't hit Wilkins, who did...might not have seen you in the street...have to call Vatterott... afraid...going to lose you..."

Kate closed her eyes and breathed deeply of Joe's special scent. Such a strong man, she thought, aware of the muscles that rippled every time he moved, and so warm. She snuggled into that warmth, wanting more of it. She shivered again.

"My God, what am I thinking?" Joe jumped up and set her on her feet. "You've got to get out of those wet things, honey." He was tugging at the blouse tucked into the waistband of her jeans.

She had the presence of mind to push his hands away. "I can do it," she said.

Joe looked doubtful but he acquiesced. "I'll start the shower for you," he offered.

"No. I can do that as well." She hurried into the bathroom, shutting the door behind her.

She let the hot stream run until the chill was gone, not bothering with soap or shampoo, but slumping against the wall of the enclosure and letting the wet heat do its magic.

By the time she returned to the bedroom, wearing the big terry robe provided by the hotel and with her head wrapped in a towel, she was feeling more normal.

Joe had ordered up a pot of coffee while she was in the bathroom, and he held a cup out to her as soon as she reentered the bedroom.

She sipped the hot, strengthening brew, eyeing Joe over the rim of the cup. He'd already shed his damp clothing and changed into dry jeans and a pullover sweater. The jeans were well worn and tight enough to outline his compelling physique, the sweater, V-necked so that she could see the strong column of his neck, the enticing mat of chest hair. His hair, only partially dried, fell in soft waves over his brow. She felt the familiar tug at her insides in response to his masculinity.

"...so it's got to be something you were involved in that you didn't realize at the time."

Kate's eyes widened as Joe's words penetrated her mind, overriding her preoccupation with his physical attributes. She hadn't registered that he was speaking.

She straightened, her back rigid, reminded that she had every good reason to suspect Joe Riley of deceit and manipulation.

"Why do you keep insisting Wilkins's death had anything to do with me?" She moved across the room to the table near the windows.

"Remember I told you that Matt wasn't working on any other case?"

"Yes. And I also recall that I suggested his murder could have been related to a case he'd been involved with before you hired him. I still think that's possible. To my mind, even probable. If I'd seen, heard or done anything to get someone this riled at me, I think I'd know it!"

She folded her arms across her chest and glared at Joe, her jaw clenched defiantly.

"Vatterott told me there was no material left in Matt's office that referred to me or you or anything to do with the investigation I hired Matt to do."

"So what? How does he know there weren't other files missing—files from previous cases? Maybe the killer, or whoever trashed Wilkins's office, just grabbed a handful of files and any notes he found lying around, which just happened to include yours."

"In that case," Joe said softly, "that car that just tried to run you down, that wasn't intentional."

Kate blinked. The memory of the brown car bearing down on her flashed into her mind with immediate and vivid intensity. The rain striking the windshield and the moving wipers had obscured the driver's face, but she had sensed his—or her—determination in that split second before Kate had regained her senses and leaped out of the way. Despite the trauma, the blur of everything before and after, she'd registered in that moment that the car had never once swerved even a fraction to avoid hitting her.

"And," Joe continued, unaware of her thoughts,

"when I had that last phone conversation with Matt, just before I heard the gunshots, he had just mentioned your name and his tone had sounded urgent. You had to have known Matt, known how laid-back and unruffled he always was, to know that tone suggested danger. Danger to you."

Kate slumped into a chair and shuddered. What if the car had met its mark? She envisioned the worst scenario; the twins being taken from the hotel and put into custody of state, told their mother was dead. Would they do an autopsy on her body, maybe discover she couldn't have been the twins' natural mother, couldn't for that matter have been the real Monica Abrigado? The twins would lose her twice, in effect. How would that impact their psyches, the rest of their lives?

"Where are the children?" she asked. "Shouldn't they be back from the park by now? Donna wouldn't have kept them out in the rain." Her voice didn't sound like her own.

Joe glanced at his watch. "I think I spotted a note on the table in the living room." He went to the door.

He returned with the note. "Donna took them down to the pool. She wrote the time down." He looked at his watch again. "We must have missed them by a few minutes."

Kate's sigh carried the tone of her relief. The children were fine. Donna was good with them, would keep them safe.

Suddenly she felt alone, vulnerable, more than ever aware of the responsibility she'd had foisted on her when she took on the babies. They had nobody but her, and at the moment, still shaken and distraught, she didn't feel up to the job.

Joe looked at Kate and saw the fear, the pain etched on her face, dulling her eyes.

He strode across the room and pulled her up into his arms, his only thought to ease the pain.

Kate slumped into his body, once again drawing comfort from his physicality. If only she could have met him under different circumstances, at another time. If only...

His hands clutched her hair, thrusting her head back, and his mouth clamped hers with an urgency that drove all thought from her mind.

She clung to him as if he were her lifeline, and suddenly he was just that, breathing life into her body with his mouth, his touch, his breathily whispered affirmations. She absorbed his scent through her skin, tasted his mouth hungrily and gave herself eagerly to his caresses.

Joe eased the robe from her shoulders, trailing kisses along her satin skin, breathing deeply of her special fragrance. "Don't tell me to stop, Katie," he whispered harshly, lifting his gaze to monitor her emotions.

She shook her head, the towel slipping downward. She dragged it off and flung it aside. "I don't want you to stop, Joe." She moaned as his tongue circled her breast. "I don't want you to ever stop." She bent back only enough to give him better access to her humming flesh.

Joe scooped her up and carried her to the bed, his hands trembling as he undid the belt and laid open the folds of the robe. She was more beautiful than he'd imagined in his fantasies of her, her body firm, her skin like porcelain. Her breasts were not large but perfectly shaped, tipped with pink nipples that had already tautened and peaked under his touch.

A growl escaped his throat as Joe bent to take one of those perfect orbs into his mouth, grazing with his teeth, lashing with his tongue. Beneath him, Kate writhed with pleasure and her hands pulled frantically at his clothing.

He pulled away only long enough to jerk his clothes from his own body, and then his hard, naked beauty was hers, offering Kate the freedom to explore every bit of his firm golden skin. Her hands stroked over his smooth back, along the hard musculature of his torso, the firm, resilient flesh that quivered under her touch.

She arched upward as his hand moved between their bodies, finding the flame-covered mound of her desire, his fingers gently parting her to learn the secrets of her femininity. Kate's bones seemed to melt under the heat that scorched her body as Joe's tongue penetrated her mouth in a rhythmic dance that echoed the movement of his fingers.

Her own hands made frantic forays over his body until one of them clasped the pulsing organ that felt like velvet to her fingers while it thrust like steel against her palm. She exploded in a sudden frenzy that almost frightened her in its magnitude, and then Joe was on top of her, her body sheathing him, limbs entwined, mouths clinging so that even their breathing seemed to come from each other's lungs.

She was everything feminine, everything joyous, her very essence succulent and seductive, and Joe wanted to bury himself within her and never resurface. And even as some part of his mind thought that, he felt the crescendo lift him upward, and his cries of rapture mingled with hers.

Kate slowly became aware of the sound of the rain against the windows, of her own panted breathing, of

Joe's soft moans of pleasure. She held him within her, loathe to be apart from him, feeling his heart thudding against her own, and she trembled with the sheer joy of the moment.

Joe felt the tremor move through her and lifted his head from the pillow beside hers. "Am I hurting you, my love?"

"No," Kate whispered, clutching him to her. "It feels so..." She hesitated, searching his face, his eyes. She saw only sweetness there, only gentle concern. "So good," she murmured, caressing his back, his buttocks, pulling him farther into herself. She gasped as she felt echoes of desire quiver within her, and at the same moment, felt Joe harden again inside of her.

There was only time for a fleeting thought that she would die if she ever had to give him up, and then all thought was swept away by feeling.

"DON'T ANSWER IT," Joe said.

"It might be Donna calling from down at the pool," Kate said, bending to kiss him before reaching for the phone.

She listened, frowned and handed the phone to Joe. "It's Detective Vatterott," she whispered.

Joe greeted the caller and grimaced at Kate. "Sure, Detective," he said, "I can be there in twenty minutes."

"What?" Kate asked, pulling the covers up to her chin as Joe got off the bed.

"Vatterott says he needs to talk to me—maybe he's got something on Matt's murder."

He pulled on his jeans, talking over his shoulder. "Will you be all right, honey? I shouldn't be gone long."

"I'll be fine. Donna should be back up with the kids soon and I'll take them down to the coffee shop for an afternoon snack."

"Okay," Joe said, his voice muffled by his shirt, "I'll look for you down there." His face emerged from the collar and he grinned at her. "Not my idea of romantic after-play but I'll make it up to you."

Kate returned his grin. "I know you will."

She heard the door latch click as he left the suite. She stretched her arms over her head, only then reminded of the aches and pains that had been pushed from her consciousness in the heat of their lovemaking. Which may have added a few more aches here and there, she thought, smiling again.

She crawled out of bed, making a sarong of the sheet, almost salivating over the thought of a hot, luxurious bubble bath. The cool air on her bare arms and shoulders brought new shivers. She went to her bag and pulled out a sweat suit. Not haute couture, but she needed warmth above all right now.

She muttered as she pushed aside clothing, looking for socks. Had she only packed a couple of pairs and worn them already? She looked around the room and spotted Joe's discarded socks on the floor beside the bed. Right. Joe would have an extra pair; he hadn't packed in a frenzied rush as she had.

She hesitated at the door to his room, suddenly shy at the idea of going through Joe's suitcase. "Like privacy is an issue at this point," she muttered as she recalled their recent intimacy.

She chuckled and crossed to the luggage rack where Joe's suitcase sat, the lid already propped halfway up by a protruding sweater. She was careful as she moved shirts and jeans, feeling around, not wanting to make a mess of his stuff. No socks. She pushed the lid all the way up and slipped her hand into the bulging cloth compartment. The top of the cloth was elasticized. As her hand closed around a pair of crew socks, her wrist pushed the elastic down. A manila envelope popped up and bounced onto the neatly stacked shirts.

Kate started to put it back, and then her glance fell on the return address stamp in the upper left corner. *Birth and Death Records?* Why would Joe have those? Was it a copy of Monica's death certificate? "But why...?"

She pulled the paper out of the envelope and stared at it, recognition dawning as she read the information relating to the birth of the twins.

She collapsed on the bed, holding the paper, trying to understand the implications. It took a moment for her mind to sort out the barrage of questions and potential explanations. But the one recurring thought pushed everything else aside.

Joe Riley was here because of the children. It was the bottom line. Everything else—Monica's death, Wilkins's death, the key, the threat of danger—was merely incidental. Joe Riley was after her children.

Flashes of memory swamped her. Images of likenesses. The jut of Joe's chin and the jut of Ashleigh's. Robbie's belly laugh, so like Joe's. The three of them making identical faces at the monkeys. God! Their eyes! How could she have missed the likeness in their eyes?

Most telling of all, Joe's immediate infatuation with the children. Grown men, bachelors, just didn't fall all over kids, bond with them, the way Joe did, in her experience. For that matter, most children didn't take to strange men the way the twins had to Joe. Did they sense the kinship at some subconscious level?

Joe Riley was the twins' father.

Kate doubled over and moaned, putting her hand to her mouth as nausea threatened. He'd come to take the children from her. Everything else was just window dressing.

She thought about what Springer had said. No threat, nobody even interested in Katelynn Adams or the Abrigado twins.

Nobody but Joe Riley.

She shoved the paper into the envelope and was about to put it back into the suitcase compartment when she was struck by another spasm of pain. She left the envelope there, snatched up her sweats and ran from the room.

If Riley was their natural father, he must be making plans to claim them legally. And this whole trip back to Manhattan must have been set in motion in order to get her and the kids back into the right jurisdiction.

She kept fumbling, wiping tears from her eyes and cheeks with the back of her hands as she dressed and shoved things into her bag, cursing under her breath at her clumsiness at a time when she most needed her wits about her. Her only thought was to get the children and get out of there before Joe Riley returned.

But another thought kept intruding, the one that kept the tears flowing despite her determination not to cry, and that was the realization that Joe had been willing to go to any lengths to keep her off guard, including making love to her.

A sob escaped as she accepted the fact that all of his subterfuge had worked. She had indeed let her guard down and, in the process, fallen in love.

"With a liar, a fake, a jerk, a bastard!"

She snatched the phone up and punched in the number marked Pool. Forcing her voice to calm, she asked for Donna, and when the sitter picked up, told her to bring the children upstairs immediately.

That done, she rushed into the bathroom carrying her bag and pushed all the cosmetics in willy-nilly. The photo of her parents was there as well, and as she pushed that forward, it fell off the counter. The glass broke as it hit the ceramic tile floor. Swearing out loud, Kate bent to pick up the pieces. She tossed them into the wastebasket and picked up the frame. Without the glass to hold the photo in place, it buckled away from the metal frame. It was just a dime-store frame. But the photo meant everything to her. She pulled it out, planning to toss the frame after the glass. Something fell out along with the picture. She bent to retrieve it and saw it was a three-by-five floppy computer disk.

She turned it over in her hands, completely baffled. How did it get there? And what was it? It had no label, nothing to indicate where it had come from, whom it belonged to, what it contained.

Joe! Joe had handled the picture last while she'd been getting ready to go out. He must have slipped it in there then. She couldn't even fathom why.

"And I don't care!" she muttered. She tossed the disk onto the back of the toilet seat, shoved picture and frame into her bag, pulled the top closed and hurried out to the living room to place it alongside the children's bag, which she'd already set next to the door.

A knock at the door startled her, but she relaxed when she realized it must be Donna with the twins.

She wiped her eyes one last time and forced a smile to her lips as she opened the door.

The two men standing there gave her no chance to react as they started to push her back inside.

"What are you…?"

A hand clamped over her mouth, an arm wrapped around her waist in an iron grip. She saw the other man turn to shut the door to the hall just as Donna loomed up in the doorway, the twins pushing around her to run into the suite.

And then she saw the gun.

Chapter Twelve

Joe's meeting with Vatterott had taken longer than he'd
anticipated. He was sure when he returned to the hotel
that Kate and the twins would already be down in the
coffee shop. They weren't. Either they'd been and gone
or they hadn't yet come down. He took the elevator up
to their floor.

When he found the door to the suite slightly ajar, he
pushed it open, expecting to be met by the noisy, happy
exuberance of healthy six-year-olds on their way out
for treats. He envisioned looking over their heads to
gaze into shining green eyes that shared the memory
of recent lovemaking.

He was met, instead, by silence.

Could he have missed them en route, going down in
one elevator while he was coming up on the other? It
wasn't like Kate to leave the door open like that,
though, as if they'd left in a hurry and hadn't bothered
to check that the latch caught.

Uneasiness churned within him.

Kate had changed her mind about the coffee shop
and taken the kids somewhere else, he told himself. In
which case, she'd have left him a note.

He looked around the sitting room and, seeing no note, went next to his own room.

The manila envelope was lying on the bed. *The unmade bed in which he'd made love with Kate.* It certainly hadn't been there when he left to meet with Vatterott. And the maid couldn't have found it and placed it there because the bed hadn't been remade.

Dread swamped him as he realized Kate had found him out, discovered the truth he'd been withholding. The irony of the timing struck him. All the way back in the cab he'd been planning to tell Kate the truth as soon as the appropriate moment presented itself. That she'd found out on her own didn't portend well for him.

Panic set in. He tore out of his room to see if she'd left a note in her room, though a sinking feeling in his stomach warned otherwise.

The door to the other bedroom opened only a couple of inches under Joe's shoulder. Something was obstructing it.

"Kate…Ash…Rob…"

Still no answer, but the door moved inward against something both soft and solid. He managed to get the door open enough to stick his head through.

Donna Milkamp lay on the floor, her body blocking the door, a red gash creasing her forehead.

Joe ran out of the suite and around to the door that led directly from the hall into the bedroom, his hand trembling so hard he could hardly get the key card into the slot. He rushed in to kneel beside the sitter.

Her pulse was thready, but when he moved her head, she moaned softly. He started to rise, to go to the phone to call 911, but just then Donna opened her eyes and weakly grasped his hand.

"I'm going to call for help," Joe assured her.

She shook her head and groaned. "No. I'm all right. Kate…the children…"

Up close he saw that the cut on her head wasn't all that deep, that the blood had dried around it, though her eyes were dull and her mouth twisted with pain as she struggled to sit up.

"Donna, are you sure…"

"Joe! Hurry. Call the police…the children…"

"Where are they, Donna?"

The effort to shake her head cost her. He could see it in her face and he gently moved her to the bed. "Two men…gun…took Kate and the twins…I couldn't…"

Joe urged her to lie down and ran to the bathroom to wet a towel. He brought it back and laid it against her forehead and then reached for the phone.

"The cops will be here shortly, Donna. Are you sure you don't want me to send down for a doctor?"

"I'm all right, Joe, really." Donna held the cloth to her head and tried to smile reassuringly.

Joe put the spread over her, just in case she was in shock, then he called the precinct. Keeping an eye on Donna, he moved restlessly around the room, punching the palm of one hand with the fist of the other as he waited for the police.

At the bathroom door he stopped, his eye caught by the shimmer of glass on the floor. He went into the room and saw the larger pieces of the glass in the wastebasket. He held the two pieces together. He recalled the framed photo of Kate and her parents at Kate's graduation. She must have dropped it.

He was about to leave the room when he spied the object on the top of the toilet tank. He picked up the floppy disk, turning it over and over in his hands, not able to identify it or understand how it came to be there. It wasn't labeled. It must be Kate's, he thought. Something she had with her from her office and left out by accident.

A pounding at the door to the suite alerted him. *Thank God.* The cops. He slipped the disk into his pocket and ran through to the living room to let them in.

"No sign of women's or kids' clothing and no bags," a plainclothes detective reported to Vatterott a few minutes later as the senior detective sat beside the bed, taking Donna's statement.

Joe sighed heavily and shut his eyes for a moment.

"Are they through in the other rooms?" Vatterott inquired.

"Just about. They'll be wanting to do this room next."

Vatterott was solicitous of the older woman as he asked if she felt up to moving into the sitting room to finish the interrogation. He and Joe each held an arm as they led her out of the bedroom and seated her on the couch in the other room.

Donna's description of the two men was fairly concise, despite the trauma of the event. "Do you think you can describe them for a police artist?" the detective asked.

"Yes."

"Think carefully now, Mrs. Milkamp. Did either of them call the other by name?"

Donna shook her head and winced. "Not that I can recall."

"Did it seem to you that Mrs....er, Ms—" he cast an irritated glance at Joe "—Ms. Abrigado...recognized either of them?"

Joe shrugged. He'd told Vatterott about Kate using Monica's name, and the detective had not been happy about this further complication to an already-complicated case.

Donna hesitated. She spoke haltingly. "We were coming off the elevator when we saw two men at the door to the suite. By the time we reached the door, both men were inside and one was about to close the door. I heard Kate say 'What are you…?' and then all hell broke loose."

Despite the discomfort she was obviously feeling, the woman blushed at her use of the word *hell*. Vatterott patted her hand and smiled.

"You're doing great, Mrs. Milkamp."

She sniffled into a tissue and nodded.

"Would you say it sounded as if she knew the guys?"

"Or maybe…surprised…that two strange men were at the door," Donna said, wishing she could be more helpful.

"Did you notice if Ms.…Kate…had packed?" he asked next.

Had she seen their bags just inside the door to the suite when they entered? She couldn't be sure; it had all happened so fast. "I…maybe…I couldn't say for certain."

She looked over at Joe then. "Why would she have packed?" she asked. "She didn't say anything to me about leaving."

Vatterott leveled a puzzled look at Joe as well.

Joe shrugged. "We had made no plans for leaving," he said. Would it help Kate and the children to tell the cops about the birth certificate, about finding it left out, proof that Kate had seen it? He didn't see how. It in no way led to what was obviously a kidnapping of the family by two strange men.

Joe stood and began pacing. He passed the windows and spotted something familiar peeking out from behind one of the drapes. He reached in and pulled out the little Santa bear Robbie carried with him everywhere. His heart plummeted and nausea threatened. He knew the police were doing their jobs in a prescribed manner, but this wasn't moving fast enough in his opinion. This wasn't the action he'd hoped for, the scouring of streets and highways, looking for Kate and the children.

As if reading his mind, Vatterott said, "We've got an APB out, Riley, and a team is already questioning employees and guests in the building. If anyone saw or heard anything meaningful, we'll know about it shortly."

But Joe needed to be doing something himself. "I've got to do something," he said aloud, bleakly eyeing the ragged-edged toy in his hands. "You've got to do more!"

"What do you think we can do that we're not already doing, Joe?" Vatterott's tone was kindly as he came over and put a sympathetic hand on Joe's shoulder. Softly he said, "It's not as if they left anything to point in their direction."

Joe knew that was so, that he was just being fractious and unreasonable out of frustration. He tossed the stuffed bear on a table and shoved his hands in his pockets to keep the others from seeing them tremble.

And felt the disk he'd found in the bathroom.

Within minutes they were down in the hotel manager's office, Joe hovering over Vatterott's shoulder as the cop slid the disk into the floppy drive of a computer.

KATE WINCED as Henry Rotterman threw the empty frame and the photo to the floor onto the pile of things he'd tossed out of their bags.

His face was flushed a deep, ominous red and beaded with an oily perspiration that flattened the thinning strands of hair against his forehead. He was panting, as though the exertion of going through her things had taken a dangerous toll on his heart. She wondered if he was about to have a heart attack, or a stroke, and if he did, would it do her any good. She tugged at the ropes at her wrists and decided it wouldn't.

"Where is the disk?" he demanded, waving the gun in his hand for emphasis.

Her jaw slackened as she gaped at the burly man who had once been her boss. "The floppy? You put it there? When? Why? How did…?"

"Don't play the Miss Innocent with me, Katelynn." Rotterman shouted over her questions. "The disk was there and now it isn't. What have you done with it?"

She shook her head. Did it really matter why these men had put it there, or what it contained? Clearly she and the children were not going to get out of here alive.

"Where are my children?" she shouted.

Rotterman went to his desk and collapsed into the chair behind it. She could see he was making an effort to calm himself. She thought it might work in her favor to keep him riled. If only she knew what they'd done with the twins, where she could find them if she managed to escape this maniac.

"Bill is taking good care of the children," Rotterman all but crooned, "and if you cooperate with us, no harm will come to them or to you." He grabbed a handful of tissues from a box on his desk and swabbed sweat from his eyes.

"Right. And after we all have tea, there's a little bridge in Brooklyn you'd like to show me," Kate scoffed, sneering at the man's pathetic attempt to con her. She made a visible effort to pull her bound wrists from the chair she was seated in. "Like you always tie up your guests before you have a friendly little visit with them."

Rotterman ground his teeth and pounded a fist on the desk, the other still pointing the gun in her direction. "I never liked your smarty attitude, girlie, and I don't like it now."

"Then shoot me," Kate said, noting with satisfaction that the man's color was rising again. He'd been grossly overweight six years ago; he was even fatter now—a sure sign that his heart was overtaxed.

She held her breath as he jerked his arm, pushing the gun inches forward in her direction.

"You want to see your kids again, you'll wise up, Katelynn. I'm running out of patience here."

"You can't let us go, Rotterman. I may have been an unwitting witness to whatever your crimes were in the past, but now you've added kidnapping to your résumé. And I'm definitely a witness to that. At least I can make sure you don't get off scot-free. The disk is in a safe place, and when I don't return, it will be handed over to the police."

She was right, she prayed. Joe would have found Donna by now and the disk in the bathroom. She marveled at the stroke of fate that led her to find the envelope in Joe's suitcase and then sent her into a frenzy of packing in order to get the children away. Rotterman and Hagar, seeing the bags near the front door, had assumed all their belongings were in them and had never searched the suite.

Now, if Joe were only smart enough to give the disk to the police, and the police could connect whatever data it contained to HRE, she and the children might yet be saved.

If Joe wasn't somehow tied up with these guys. She didn't want to believe that. But somehow he seemed to have led them right to her. Could that have been a coincidence? She'd only know if he managed to find her, before Rotterman could do his worst.

But meanwhile, she had to stall for time.

"When did you put the disk behind the picture?" she asked.

"What difference does it make?"

Kate shrugged, pretending an indifference she didn't feel. "None, I suppose, but maybe if you told me what this was all about, I'd feel more...uh...well, maybe I could see your side of things. Be more willing to co-operate."

She controlled the urge to smile when she saw her ex-boss grasping at the phony straw she'd offered.

He mopped at his face again and settled back in his chair.

"The treasury department got an anonymous tip about some things we were...into."

For a moment Kate almost thought he was embarrassed to admit to his criminal activities despite the fact that he was now guilty of kidnapping and probably murder. She had to swallow at the thought that he probably intended to add her death and the children's to his list of crimes. But she kept her expression even and nodded sympathetically so he'd continue speaking.

"They raided us in the middle of a workday. It so happened Bill was in your office, using your computer to update the special file he kept and..."

"Special file?" Kate interrupted. She was puzzled. If he'd used the house computer, why hadn't she ever come across the file? "Mr. Rotterman, I used that computer all day, every day. If there'd been an extra file in there, I'd have seen it."

Rotterman shook his head, a look of admiration crossing his face. "Bill Hagar knew what he was doing, all right. He had a system. He used the computer during your lunch hour or after you'd gone for the day. After he updated, he'd transfer it all to a backup disk and erase the work on the hard drive, so there was never any evidence left for you to stumble across."

Kate frowned. "Are you talking about a second set of books?" It was the only thing she could think of that the IRS would be interested in.

Rotterman nodded. "Something like that."

"And that disk you put into my picture frame, that was the one Hagar had the file on?"

"Yeah. He heard the agents storm the building just seconds after he'd done the backup. He managed to erase the file from the hard drive, but didn't dare be caught with the backup disk on him. He knew the agents would tear the place apart looking for evidence. He saw that picture you always kept on your desk and stuck it there.

"Pretty smart of him, I always thought. It kept the agents from finding it because they let all of you come back into the building to collect your personal stuff. They never even considered the picture, and you took it with you."

He sighed, remembering what came later.

"We thought we'd be able to put our hands on it whenever we wanted. We had your address, never figured you for up and leaving town, just disappearing like that."

Kate was beginning to understand everything now. "And that disk was all that stood between you and a conviction," she said softly.

"We tried to find you, thinking you'd discover it and turn it over to the cops when your read the data—or maybe even come after us to pay for its return."

"You thought I'd blackmail you?" Kate's voice was shrill, surprising even her. After all, thinking her capable of such a thing was the least of this man's assaults on her. Besides, wasn't it a truism that dishonest people always suspected everyone else of dishonesty?

Her laugh was heavy with irony. "I'd never have done that, you know."

Rotterman shrugged, ignoring her protest. "When months went by and we couldn't find you and didn't hear from you, we figured we were safe. Told ourselves there'd never be any reason for you to take the picture out of the frame and find the thing. It wasn't until that private dick came around asking questions that we started to worry all over again."

He opened his desk drawer, pawing around inside, and closed it with a disgruntled slam. Kate wondered what he was looking for, but she didn't ask. Instead she asked the question that had been bothering her since she faced the two men in her doorway.

"How did you know where to find me?" she asked.

Rotterman laughed, a nasty, raucous sound. "Somebody hired a private eye to do our hunting for us. All we had to do was follow the hunter."

So Rotterman or Hagar had killed Wilkins. Kate's

breath quivered in her throat as she realized she hadn't been taking this man seriously enough. Whatever was on that disk, it was enough to motivate him to murder. Another thought brought a sense of relief despite the gravity of her situation. Rotterman had said "Somebody hired a private eye," implying that he didn't know who that person was, that Joe wasn't connected to Rotterman and Hagar. At least, she'd go to her death knowing Joe wasn't one of the bad guys.

Rotterman wasn't through, it seemed.

"Funny thing is, we'd given up thinking of you as a possible threat. If some jerk who was looking for his kids hadn't hired that P.I., you'd have stayed underground and we'd have gone about our business with no interest in you whatsoever. Fact is, we couldn't take any chances on you stumbling over the disk if you surfaced again. But you're sort of like that proverbial bad penny, girlie."

He roared at his little joke until the laughter turned to a coughing fit and he had to struggle to get his breathing evened out again.

"But how did you find me at the hotel?" Kate asked when he recovered himself.

"Hagar's girlfriend took care of that for us." When he shook his head, his jowls shook as well.

"Hagar's girlfriend?"

Rotterman chortled. "That scrawny Maynard bitch. I never did see what he saw in her, but she came through for us when we lost you after you hauled ass out of Lake George."

Kate paled and felt her stomach lurch as she realized she'd openly given her whereabouts to Terri Maynard, who'd questioned her under the guise of friendship.

So now she knew all of it. Would she ever be able to trust anyone again as long as she lived?

And despite the fact that Rotterman had taken his time telling her, the cavalry hadn't shown up to save her, so the question as to the length of time she would live was becoming moot.

In desperation she tried one more ploy.

"I was telling you the truth, Rotterman. I found that disk long ago and gave it to a friend for safekeeping in case you ever came after me. If I don't show up with the children, within a few days, my friend has orders to submit the evidence to the cops."

She watched his features twist into a grimace of doubt. With a sinking heart, she saw doubt replaced by disbelief.

"You're bluffing. It won't work. I'll just give you a little time to think about it and how maybe you can even save the lives of those kids."

He got up and left the room. He was starving. Stress did that to him. A little snack was in order while Miss Smartypants cooled her heels and thought about the trouble she was in and realized she had nothing to gain by stalling. Anticipation was another thing that made him hungry.

Chapter Thirteen

"I don't like it here," Robbie said, looking around the huge, gloomy boathouse where the paddlewheelers were brought for repairs. "I want my mommy."

"Hey, this room's got some great features," Hagar defended. He didn't know why he got stuck with the baby-sitting and Henry got to deal with the woman. Besides, he knew he'd do better getting information out of Katelynn Adams than his partner would. Who died and left Rotterman boss, anyway? He would have been the obvious one to lead the operation if Rotterman hadn't gotten his fat hands on the gun first.

Ashleigh sniffed with disdain. "Who cares. I want Mommy now. I don't like you and I don't like that bad man with the gun."

"Mr. Rotterman was just joking," Hagar said. "The gun is just make-believe. You know, like a toy gun."

"I saw real guns at the police station," Ashleigh said, "and that is not a toy gun, neither."

"Yeah," Robbie added, "that ain't no toy gun, neither. I got lotsa toy guns and that ain't one."

"Robbie," his sister said primly, "you only have one toy gun—not lots—and you know Mommy and Marybeth told you not to say 'ain't.'"

Hagar chuckled. "Little boys who lie go to hell," he warned, winking at Ashleigh.

Both children stared up at him, mouths agape. "You said a bad word," Robbie gasped.

"Ooh, your mommy's going to be so mad at you," Ashleigh intoned. "You won't have any treats for…for a long, long time."

"Yeah, a lo-o-ong time," Robbie added.

"I want to go back to my mommy now," Ashleigh stated firmly.

"She's still talking to my partner," Hagar told them.

"I don't care. I'm going back." Robbie started for the door on the other side of the cavernous repair room.

"Me, too." His sister started after him.

"Wait." Hagar ran and grabbed Ashleigh's arm. "Get back here," he ordered, speaking to Robbie's back, "or I'll have to hurt your sister."

Robbie turned around, his eyes widening in a mix of fear and outrage.

"You leave my sister alone," he yelled, running back toward them.

"Come on," Hagar said, keeping a hold on Ashleigh's arm, "I want to show you something."

He didn't care what Rotterman said, he was through baby-sitting. They couldn't let the woman or the kids go, anyway. It was time to get rid of some deadweight.

He pulled Ashleigh over to the wall and pulled down a lever in the wall. The old floorboards started creaking as the two sections parted, revealing the lake water underneath, and at the same time the huge door at the end of the room began rising. When a boat was brought in for repair, a hydraulic hoist a few feet under the water could be activated to lift it up to dry dock.

"See, it's like a swimming pool," Hagar purred, trying to get the children to relax.

"Is not," Robbie said, drawing nearer. "It's so they can drive the boats in for repairs."

"How'd you know that?" Hagar was really surprised by the boy's knowledge.

"They got one at the marina where Mommy's boats go," Ashleigh said, still trying to tug out of Hagar's grasp.

"Yes, but this is different, we have…um…dolphins in our water."

"Dolphins?" Robbie edged closer, his eyes saucer-like.

"I'll bet you don't," Ashleigh said.

"Real dolphins?" the little boy asked.

"Yep. The real McCoy. Look! I think you can see one over there."

Robbie almost ran to the edge of the opening and Hagar was ready for him. He grabbed the boy's arm and jerked him to his side.

JOE'S NERVES WERE screaming by the time Detective Vatterott pulled into the parking lot of the bar and grill located across the street from HRE. The detective had radioed ahead to the Yonkers PD, asking to be met there, but so far there was no sign of anyone else in the deserted lot.

"We may not have a lot of time," Joe protested for the umpteenth time. "We should go in now."

Vatterott lit a cigarette, opening his window to let the smoke out. His manner was infuriatingly calm in Joe's opinion. "Not my jurisdiction here. Have to wait for the locals to go in."

"What about probable cause?" Joe demanded, repeating something he'd read in a novel or heard on TV.

"Still have to have the Yonkers Police Department."

"What if they've gone through her stuff and discovered the disk isn't there? They could…"

Radio static interrupted Joe's argument and he held his breath as Vatterott snatched up the handset and pressed the button. The dispatcher's voice informed the NYC detective that the team that was supposed to meet him had been held up and would be there in fifteen minutes.

"Fifteen minutes!" Joe exploded. "They could be dead in fifteen minutes."

He jerked the car handle up and jumped out of the car before Vatterott could discard his cigarette and get his own door open.

Joe heard the detective shouting for him to come back as he dashed across the road and ran around the side of the HRE building, looking for any means of entry.

THEY WERE LIKE a couple of snakes, writhing, spitting, twisting in his grip and slippery as hell. They'd kicked and bitten him and the little girl almost slipped out of his grasp a couple of times, but Hagar held on, determined that when he got rid of them, it would be final. They were brats who deserved what he had in store for them.

His grip on the boy tightened as he saw that he had the kid right at the edge of the floor opening. With a mighty thrust of energy he flung the boy forward and let go, turning immediately to grab the girl's flailing arm with his free hand.

Ashleigh heard Robbie's scream, heard the splash as he hit the water, and her own scream echoed in terror. She had to get away from the bad man, had to save Robbie. She kicked out as hard as she could, wishing she was wearing her Mary Janes instead of sneakers. It hurt her foot whenever she kicked him and didn't seem to hurt him very much at all. Her wrists burned where the man was holding them, and they hurt more when she tried to twist away.

Hagar danced the girl in a circle, holding his body out to keep her kicks from doing any real damage as he tried to get her back over to the edge of the opening.

She was a feisty brat and strong for a little kid. He'd had enough. He let go with his right hand, balled it into a fist and hit her with all his greater strength and determination behind the punch.

She seemed to fly through the air, landing with a sickening thud on the cement housing of the compressor unit. He heard her head crack against the sharp corner, saw the blood spurt from the wound.

He started toward her, panic shooting through him. He needed to get her in the water where the evidence would make it look like she'd hit her head when she fell in. It had to look like they'd drowned. Like an accident.

The sound from behind him was so inhuman it was unrecognizable; something between a roar and a scream that deafened him as a great weight fell against his back, bringing him crashing to the floor. Hands of steel gripped his head, pounding it on the floor, and the last thought Hagar had before he blacked out was that Rotterman always got the easy jobs.

Joe was out of breath as he spun around and ran to the edge of the water. Robbie was fighting furiously, gasping, choking, screaming, his cries echoing in the cavernous room, his arms flailing helplessly, as Joe jumped over the side and reached for him. For a minute he thought he was going to have to knock the boy out in order to subdue him enough to get a good grip on him. He yelled for Robbie to calm down, that it was him, Joe, that he'd save him. He could see the boy was tiring, that in his frenzy he was swallowing great gulps of water. Joe could feel his own shoes filling with water, pulling him down. He kicked them off and grabbed the boy, easing him around until he could get his arms around Robbie's shoulders.

It seemed forever before he got the boy to the edge of the opening, though it was only a few feet. Robbie hadn't stopped struggling for a minute, and Joe's arms ached from the effort to hold on with one arm and stroke with the other.

He gasped as he laid the boy down on the floor and knelt over him, pushing on Robbie's chest to expel some of the water the kid had swallowed. He grunted with satisfaction when the boy doubled over and began vomiting on the floor.

And now he had to find the others. Kate and Ashleigh. Even as he thought that, his glance fell on the compressor unit. He saw the dangling legs clad in pink jeans, the bottoms of the little sneakers, one pink-sweatered arm hanging limply over the edge of the block, lifeless.

He stood up, his eyes glazing over with grief.

He was too late. They'd already killed Ashleigh.

His cry of anguish echoed and reechoed as he stumbled to his feet and ran to his little girl.

THE MINUTE ROTTERMAN LEFT his office, Kate began working her arms up over the back of the chair, easing up out of the seat inch by careful inch. It seemed to take forever, but the fact that her feet were unbound and the rope had some give to it enabled her to finally work loose from the chair. Now she had only to figure out some way to get her wrists free from the ropes; not an easy task with them bound behind her. For a moment she stood stock-still, overcome by a sense of futility.

An image of the children, laughing, running free in the playground, flashed into her mind. Of course she could get free; all she had to do was use her head. She made a careful survey of the room, constantly twisting her wrists as she gazed around. Did she only imagine they felt looser? She kept working them.

Rotterman's office, never a hive of business activity in her memory, seemed to offer little in the way of tools. There weren't even the regulation pieces of office equipment. Except for the desk, the room seemed more a reflection of Rotterman's ownership than his business acumen. There was a pinball machine on one wall, and a TV set with a VCR on a stand in the corner near the door. A playroom for an overgrown child.

Kate studied those items, trying to figure a way to use them to break free, but they seemed useless for the purpose.

She went to the desk, hoping something on the surface would lend itself to the task. "Oh, Kate, you dummy," she gasped as she stood looking down at the phone. How could she have overlooked the obvious?

She bent forward at the waist and knocked the phone set off the cradle with her face. She tried to hit the first of the three emergency numbers with her nose and only succeeded in bruising it. She drew back and took a deep breath, ignoring the tears that the bump on her nose had brought on.

It was then that she realized she wasn't hearing a dial tone. Had she inadvertently activated a number? She bent forward again and tried to push the button on the cradle. She managed to hit it, but it didn't raise the tone.

She slumped against the edge of the desk, discouraged. How much time had she wasted trying to dial 911? Rotterman could return at any moment and she was no closer to freeing herself than she'd been when he left.

She made another survey of the room. A prism of light caught her eye as she turned her head. She swung around and stared at the cabinet that contained Rotterman's collection of beer mugs. The cabinet had a glass door.

It was with vengeful satisfaction that Kate aimed a foot at the glass. The glass broke inward, leaving sharp corners remaining in the frame, cutting her ankle in the process. She ignored the sudden pain, the warm flow of blood, and spun around, looking over her shoulder as she backed up to guide her bound wrists to the broken glass.

ROTTERMAN HEARD THE SOUNDS of children shouting and Hagar's bellows over that. He carried the sandwich he was eating to the door of the snack room and leaned out into the hall, listening. He could hear that they were in the repair room, the acoustics in there making the sounds reverberate so they seemed exaggerated. He shrugged and went on munching. Nothing to worry about. Hagar could handle a couple of brats.

He went back into the room and plugged some coins

into the pop machine and then punched the button for fruit punch. The Sold Out message lit up. Grumbling, he took another huge bite of the sandwich and hit the root beer button. Another Sold Out message. He kicked the machine, swore viciously, and hit all the buttons one after another. Nothing happened.

He looked around the room for something to pry the door open, positive that the machine wasn't actually empty, but merely out of order. Before he could find anything, he became aware that the noise from the repair room had escalated. Muttering expletives, he went to see what all the commotion was about.

KATE HELD THE LARGE, heavy metal beer stein in her hand and crept along the hall in the direction of the noise. She'd cut her wrists in the process of cutting the ropes, her face hurt from her fiasco with the phone, and her ankle was throbbing. The aches and pains seemed to give her fresh energy rather than slowing her down. She had just turned the corner, was two doors down from the snack room, when she saw Rotterman come out, the gun shoved in his back pocket. She bit back a cry of surprise and swiftly moved back around the corner. If he was returning to the office he'd be coming this way. Should she run back to the office and wait for him there?

And then she heard a terrible cry of pain that was like the anguished bellow of a wounded elephant. It came from the repair room at the end of the hall and she heard Rotterman's footsteps running toward it.

She sped around the corner, unmindful of the noise she made, knowing only that one of her family was hurt.

Ahead of her she saw Rotterman stop to pull the gun from his pocket before reaching out to turn the handle.

Kate took a deep breath and leaped forward, the beer stein held over her head with both hands.

VATTEROTT AND TWO UNIFORMS from YPD found Joe Riley and a little boy huddled over the still form of a little girl. Blood covered the child's face, her clothing and the cement block she lay on. Man and boy were soaking wet, but Vatterott could still see the tears that slid down their faces.

"Call an ambulance," Joe croaked.

One of the cops was already calling it in on his radio phone while another had pulled the lever to close the floor sections over the water.

Suddenly a door crashed open and a hulk of a man fell forward into the room, a gun flying out of his hand to land on the floor and slide into the water just before the sections met in the middle.

Behind the fallen man, a woman rushed into the room, leaping over the man she'd struck from behind, her eyes wide with terror. She spun around, saw the body of the little girl on the compressor unit, saw Riley and the little boy kneeling beside it, and fell in a dead faint only a few feet from where Vatterott stood.

A quart-size metal beer stein fell from her hand, bounced on the floor and then rolled away, clinking its progress across the room until it came to a stop against the wall.

At almost the same moment, a chopping noise was heard overhead and from another door, four men in suits burst into the room, weapons ready to fire. Above all the sound, an ambulance siren blared as it ap-

proached the building and then whined to a halt when
the vehicle screeched into place outside the door.

Detective Peter Vatterott of the NYPD shook his
head and went to revive Katelynn Adams. If they ever
managed to sort through this mess, to come out of it
with no fatalities and with all the answers falling into
place, he planned to take a long overdue vacation and
try for the umpteenth time to quit smoking.

The woman stirred as he gently slapped her cheek.
"Ms. Adams," he said softly, "I'm Detective Vatterott. Are you all right?" He'd seen the cuts on her wrists
and the blood that soaked the right leg of her jeans.
His question was moot. She was going to need first aid,
at least.

"Wh-what…?"

"You fainted, Ms. Adams," Vatterott said.

Kate remembered. "Ash…Ashleigh?"

She jerked away from the detective and bolted to her
feet, swaying for a moment as another surge of dizziness swept over her.

She couldn't see past the circle of bodies around the
compressor. Paramedics, men in plainclothes, uni-
formed cops. She pushed past the men to reach the little
girl.

One of the paramedics grabbed her arm and pulled
her back as another placed an oxygen mask over Ashleigh's deathly pale face. As he moved back, Kate
could see the blood spattered all over the child's clothing and down the cement housing of the unit. A hand
gripped her shoulder as her legs threatened to give way
again. She turned and found herself held against Joe's
hard chest. She pulled away, looking for Robbie.

One of the paramedics had wrapped him in a blanket

and was carrying him to the door where the ambulance was parked. Kate ran after them.

"Mommy," Robbie called weakly when she came up beside him. His arms reached out to her and the paramedic relinquished the damp bundle into Kate's desperate embrace.

"Ash got kilt, Mommy," the little boy cried, his hands frantically clawing at her. "The man kilt her! He kilt her!" His body was shaking with terror, his face wet with tears, his eyes huge with anguish. He struggled in her arms, almost as if he were frantic to get away from the painful knowledge that he'd lost his sister.

"No, Robbie, shh. No! She isn't dead," Kate intoned, praying she was telling the truth. "They're taking care of her right now, and she's going to be all right."

She set him down on the open tailgate of the ambulance and took his face in her hands, forcing him to meet her eyes, to quiet himself enough to hear her words.

She saw him struggle to believe her, felt his body start to relax. She watched his face change to accept her promise.

"Got to move, lady," a voice urged behind her. She lifted Robbie into her arms and moved back, holding her breath, fighting her own terror as the paramedics moved the stretcher holding Ashleigh's still form into the vehicle.

Robbie reached out, trying to touch his sister. Kate grabbed his arm and held it against her chest; she fought back the scream that threatened to tear from her throat.

A tall, thin, young-looking woman in a dark blue

rescue uniform reached for Robbie. "We'll take him now, ma'am. We need to take his vitals. You can ride with us to the hospital."

She sat on the floor between the two gurneys, holding a hand of each of her children, one gripping hers for reassurance, the other limp and frighteningly cold. The female paramedic handed her some tissues. Kate wiped her eyes and blew her nose, but the tears continued to fall and finally she stopped trying to blot them away.

"I'LL TAKE YOU to the hospital, Joe," Vatterott said, keeping an arm along Joe's shoulders, guiding him toward the parking lot. Across the way he saw the federal agents arguing with the YPD over jurisdiction, the two prisoners handcuffed to each other, standing between the vehicles of the two groups.

Vatterott chuckled. "Wait until they find out the NYPD has a claim on them," he said. "It's going to be a three-ring circus. Literally."

Joe clenched his teeth. He could care less how it all went down. He just needed to get to the hospital, needed to see Ashleigh, to know they were doing everything they could to save her. He stumbled and felt Vatterott grip his arm to steady him.

"I'm all right," he muttered, reaching eagerly for the door handle of the detective's car. "Let's just get there," he pleaded.

It was nearly impossible for Joe to keep his emotions in check on the interminably long ride to the hospital. It seemed as if Vatterott hit every red light, and Joe wanted to scream at the man just to drive through, heedless of the law, of the danger. He didn't feel the tears that continuously slid down his cheeks, didn't hear the moans that escaped his throat every few minutes, wasn't aware of the shivers that shook his body under his damp clothing.

Vatterott glanced over at his passenger, wondering if the man was in shock. If there hadn't been such urgency to get the little girl to the hospital, he'd have insisted the paramedics check Joe's vitals. As it was, he cranked up the car heater and wished he'd driven a patrol car with a siren instead of his own beat-up Mercury.

He breathed a sigh of relief as he spotted the hospital ahead and then pulled into the emergency drive. Riley was out of the car before it came to a complete stop. Vatterott ran after him, unmindful of the fact that he'd left the car in a no-parking zone.

Inside, chaos prevailed as doctors and nurses rushed to attend to the various medical needs of the Abrigado family. He could hear Kate's voice quivering with indignation as a nurse begged her to leave Ashleigh's side and let them do their work, while an intern argued that she needed medical attention herself.

When Joe joined the fracas, all hell broke loose.

"I'm going in to see my child," he was shouting, attempting to push past the medical team while Robbie was screaming for Kate as two nurses pushed his gurney into another cubicle.

A nurse whose name tag announced that she was both Mrs. Kyley, and ER Nursing Supervisor managed to calm Joe by sternly announcing they were going to need blood donations for Ashleigh. Vatterott stepped forward, wanting to warn that Riley was probably in shock himself, but decided they'd find that out when they took his vitals before drawing blood. Instead, he went to a coffee machine, drew himself a cup of caffeine and sat down to wait it out.

He had dozed off when he was startled awake by a hand on his arm.

Katelynn Adams removed the half-empty cup from his hands and sat down beside him. Her wrists and ankle were bandaged, her clothing bloodied and wrinkled. Her eyes were shadowed, and lines of fatigue and stress pulled at her mouth.

"You're Detective Vatterott?" she asked, attempting to smile at him.

"Peter…Pete. You're all right?"

She grimaced. "As all right as I can be under the circumstances." Her eyes slanted toward the emergency room doors.

"Any news yet?"

"They're taking her up to surgery," Kate said, swallowing with obvious difficulty.

"How's the little boy?"

"He's sleeping. They gave him a mild sedative."

She didn't seem to realize she was holding the cup, Vatterott took it from her hands and tossed it into a waste receptacle. "Can I get you something? Some hot tea?"

"Thank you."

Vatterott went back to the machine and punched the buttons for hot tea and extra sugar. When he carried it back to Kate, he saw the vulnerability in her eyes. Something more than fear for the little girl was present in the look.

"What about Joe?" he asked.

Kate reached for the cup with trembling hands. "He's donating blood, I think."

"Do you feel up to answering a few questions?" Vatterott asked as he sat back down beside her.

Kate shrugged. "Whatever."

The detective winced at the monotone in that single word. The fight suddenly seemed to have gone out of her. It didn't jibe with what he knew about her. Was it when he mentioned Riley?

He cleared his throat, suddenly unsure of himself. Maybe this should wait. After all he wasn't even here in an official capacity. At least not until it was worked out who got first shot at the Rotterman-Hagar duo. Mostly he needed to satisfy his own curiosity.

He patted Kate's shoulder. "I'm sure she's going to be fine, Ms. Adams."

Kate nodded and closed her eyes. An image of Ashleigh, lying on the compressor unit, covered in blood, came into her mind. And then she remembered hearing Joe shout "My child."

So he'd finally admitted his paternity. And with those words, she knew her life had ended.

She felt the detective's movement beside her, heard him chuckle. Her eyes popped open and she turned to stare at him.

"Sorry," he said with the remnants of a smile on his lips. "I was just thinking about how Riley was like a bear smelling a picnic nearby when we got to HRE. There was no holding him back when he thought you and the children were at risk."

Just the children, Kate amended silently. Not me. I was just a means to an end.

She shrugged and turned, without comment, to look down the long hall to the double doors that allowed no admission beyond that point. Beyond those doors Ashleigh was fighting for her life.

The doctors had assured her, following the CAT scan, that there'd been no internal damage, but the gash to her head was deep and required surgical repair. She had a concussion and would need to be observed for a couple of days, too. And of course there'd been considerable blood loss.

As if reading her mind, Detective Vatterott said, "Head wounds usually bleed profusely—it often looks worse than it is."

Again Kate nodded without speaking. She had a question for the detective, but didn't know if she could trust herself not to burst into tears if she asked it. She didn't care for herself, but she did care that the last image the twins had of her might be in cuffs.

She sipped the tea that was now lukewarm and too sweet, but it wet her mouth.

She leveled a grave look at Vatterott, cleared her throat and asked huskily, "Am I going to be under arrest for taking the children?"

Chapter Fourteen

Vatterott's jaw slackened. He hadn't expected the question; it had honestly never entered his mind that there might be a question of criminal charges against the woman who had taken Monica Abrigado's children and sheltered them from what she perceived to be a real threat to them.

If this was what was bothering Katelynn Adams, he could put her mind at rest.

"Hey," he said, taking her hand, "nobody can fault you for doing what their mother asked you to do. Besides," he said with what he hoped was an encouraging smile, "who is there to press charges?"

Kate's expression remained grave. "Their father?"

"Their…? Oh!"

But surely Joe Riley wasn't going to make trouble for the woman who'd cared for the children all these years with nothing to gain from it but their best welfare. Besides, he'd got the impression that Riley had a definite yen for this woman. And who could blame him? Even an old, married square like Pete Vatterott could appreciate her beauty. Even now, disheveled, distraught, her face pinched with worry and fatigue, her loveliness shone through. No, he didn't see Riley doing something stupid and screwing up any chance he had to have a relationship with Katelynn Adams.

He smiled and patted Kate's hand. "This is no time to worry about what will most likely never occur. You need to concentrate on those two little tykes right now. Everything else will work itself out."

"Thank you," she said, though she wasn't so sure he was right about things working out. How could they? Joe would want to take the children to live with him. And that would leave her...

"Ms. Abrigado?"

Meggie, the nurse who'd cleaned her cuts and bandaged them, had come up to them. "They've moved Ashleigh to recovery. She'll be going up to the peds unit in about—" Meggie glanced at her watch "—about twenty minutes. They put Robbie in the other bed. Dr. Carlton thought it would be good for them to be together. It's Room 234."

Kate jumped up, anxious to be there when Ashleigh came around.

"You're going to stay?" she asked the detective.

"I'll wait for Joe, tell him the good news," Vatterott said, settling back comfortably.

Robbie was drifting between waking and dozing when Kate tiptoed into the room. He opened his eyes and gave her a fuzzy smile. "Hi, Mommy," he murmured.

"Hi, my love. How are you feeling?" She sat on the edge of the bed and ran her hand over his soft, dark curls.

"Sleepy."

She laughed softly. "Yeah. They gave you some good medicine so you'd be able to rest."

"I drowneded, Mommy," he whimpered, rousing himself, his little face earnest.

"No, honey, you didn't drown. Joe saved you, remember?"

Robbie's face lit up. "He did? That's so cool."

"Cool," she agreed, smiling.

He was quiet for a moment, and she saw that he was drifting off again. She continued to stroke his hair back from his forehead, more aware than she'd ever been of how precious he was to her.

"Boy…Joe must really love me…to save m…"

His words ended in the little snorting sound Robbie made when he fell asleep.

The tears fell hot and heavy then, her head bent with the weight of her pain. How would she ever bear losing this child? And his twin? They'd been her very center for more than five years—the blessing she woke up to every morning, the subject of her prayers every night.

She caressed the dimpled little hand that still bore the plump softness of babyhood. In another year or so, the twins' hands would be leaner, the fingers longer, the baby look gone. Their round faces would begin to show their bone structure, their speech patterns lose the childish inflections and the cute mispronunciations. But she wouldn't be there to see the changes.

She heard a sound at the door and snatched a tissue out of the box on the bedside table.

They were bringing Ashleigh in. Kate stood up, still drying her eyes, and waited until they'd transferred the little girl from gurney to bed.

When the medical staff had left the room, promising to check back shortly, Kate stood at the side of the bed, holding on to the side rail, looking down at the unconscious child.

Ashleigh's curls had been shaved from one side and there was a bandage swathing her head, giving her a rakish appearance.

Ashleigh would love the look. Kate could see her standing in front of a mirror, burlesquing a pirate's stance. And of course she'd lord it over Robbie, who had no bandages to show for his own traumatic experience.

She reached over the rail and gingerly touched the curls, so like her brother's, on the left side of Ashleigh's head.

She tried to imagine Joe on his own with the children. Sure, he was great with them when she was there, but how would he fare when Ash refused to have her hair combed, just because, as she would say, "I'm not in the mood"? Or when she threw every single thing she owned, from shelves, closet and dresser, out into the hall and announced with grim satisfaction that she was "tired of all this junk." Would Joe know enough to wait her out, or would he be one of those parents who insisted she clean up her mess immediately, demanding she submit to parental authority even at the cost of her own budding personality? Would he know enough to make sure that when Ashleigh hauled everything back, she believed it was her own idea?

And Robbie, still clinging to some of the baby habits of five while awkwardly attempting to emulate his idea of seven. Would Joe demand he stop being a baby even though Robbie wasn't quite ready to make the transition? Would he expect Robbie to play only with "boy" toys and give up his beloved stuffed animals?

It was all moot, anyway, wasn't it, she thought, pulling the cover up higher on Ashleigh's chest. Joe Riley was their natural parent, and she was not.

She turned as an intern came into the room, warming the metal piece on his stethoscope in his palm. A nurse came in behind him and smiled pleasantly.

"We're going to examine Ashleigh now, Mrs. Abrigado. Would you mind going out to the parents' waiting room? I'll call you when we're done."

Kate looked over to see that Robbie was still sleeping and tiptoed out.

She was about to turn the corner into the parents' waiting room when she heard Joe speaking with someone.

Not ready to face him, Kate froze in place.

"The children are adopted, eh?"

"What are you talking about?" Joe asked, his voice nearly a gasp.

"Uh, well, according to the blood matches we did for Ashleigh, it's obvious neither you nor Ms. Abrigado is the natural parent of the twins."

Kate stifled her own gasp and slumped against the wall.

"That's not possible! You've made a mistake. Check again. You've got the blood samples mixed up or something. I'm their father. You've made a mistake!" Joe was shouting, heedless of the occupants of the waiting room behind him. The pain in his voice was palpable.

"I'm sorry, sir. These are the right tests." There was a pause and then he said, "But surely you knew…"

There was a flurry of footsteps and Joe came running around the corner, passing within inches of Kate pressed against the wall.

He didn't see her. She saw that his face was flushed, his eyes swimming with tears. He ran down the hall, toward the exit door.

Kate looked after him, her own eyes burning, her stomach lurching with empathy.

He loved the twins. He wasn't their father after all, but he loved them. It wasn't a matter of blood, of a legal claim to them; he loved them for themselves, unconditionally.

His pain seemed to stream behind him, connecting to her heart, to her mind. She could feel it coursing through her blood.

"Oh, Ms. Abrigado, I was just coming to tell you that you could return to the children's room."

The nurse touched her arm. "Ms. Abrigado, did you hear me? I said you can…"

"Yes. Yes, of course, thank you." Kate rushed past the nurse, hoping to catch Joe before he left the hospital. But halfway down the hall she stopped, realizing that Joe might prefer to be alone to work through his disappointment without anyone witnessing his anguish.

She'd probably be the last person he wanted to see right now, anyway. After all, he might feel some embarrassment about their recent lovemaking in light of the fact that it wasn't going to…

Confusion made chaos of her train of thought. What had he expected to gain by making love to her? What difference could it make to his ultimate claim on the children, had it turned out they were really his? But then, that was it, wasn't it? At the time, he'd only supposed—hoped—they were his. He was trying to keep her distracted until he could gain proof.

She turned and made her way slowly back to the children's room. How did Joe expect to get that proof when the birth certificate clearly stated "father unknown"?

The key! Did he think the key would unlock some

kind of journals or papers of Monica's that named him as father? That made sense to her. He'd certainly been more than willing to risk his neck to get his hands on that key.

But then, why agree so immediately when she suggested turning the key over to Springer?

She looked up at the number on a door and realized that in her preoccupation, she'd gone past room 234. She turned and made her way back.

It was silly to torment herself with questions she didn't have answers to. She needed to take Detective Vatterott's advice and focus on the children. It dawned on her that with the danger gone, they were free to go home, to resume their normal lives in Lake George.

Thinking of home reminded her of Marybeth. All of a sudden she could hardly wait to curl up in bed with a telephone and tell her best friend everything that had gone down in the past few days. And Marybeth would present an objective ear; she'd help Kate sort it all out.

But just as she put her hand on the door to the children's room, a flash of clarity lit up her mind.

What if the children had been Joe's? Would she be going through this door now, or would Joe have made his move and already pushed her out of their lives?

JOE TOOK A LAST LOOK around the room, making sure he hadn't forgotten anything. For that matter, the past week had proved he could subsist on next to nothing. He'd checked into a motel on the edge of Yonkers with no luggage and spent the whole week there without a change of clothes or a shave. For a generous tip, the waitress at the greasy spoon adjacent to the motel had been more than willing to deliver coffee and hamburgers, the mainstay of his diet during that week, since he hadn't had the impetus to make decisions, even about his menu. He hadn't left the room at all until this morning.

"Come on, Riley," he said aloud. "You know you haven't forgotten anything."

A nasty thought surfaced in the back of his mind. *Just your heart, Riley. But no biggie.*

For a moment his gaze lingered on the bed remembering another bed where he'd made love to Kate. As if mesmerized by the memory, he went back to the bed and ran his hand over the surface of it. If he closed his eyes he could see Kate lying there, her skin glowing like perfectly glazed porcelain, her flame-colored hair seeming to set fire to the pillowcase as it fanned out around her head. His hand caressed the bedspread, almost feeling the curve of her breast, the warmth of her flesh, the tremors that shook her as she responded to his kisses.

He bit his lip and opened his eyes. This was self-defeating. And painful as hell.

Angrily he snatched up his suitcase and headed out the door, determined to restore his life to some semblance of order in the couple of weeks he had left before he reported back to work.

He returned the car to the rental agency and then caught a cab to the hotel he'd been staying at before he left for Lake George. The desk clerk remembered him and offered him the same room. He took it telling himself it would be like returning home. It wasn't. Being with Kate and the twins had been home. He pushed the thought away. He couldn't let himself think about Kate and the twins, couldn't function unless he cleared his mind of the past.

He called Vatterott because he'd promised to check in and leave his phone number.

"The D.A. is still arguing priority on the Wilkins murder," the detective told him, "and the Justice Department is arguing prior claim." He laughed heartily. "Yonkers is making a half-assed bid for attempted murder and the FBI wants them on kidnapping. All in all, it looks like the Terrible Two don't have a corner to hide in."

"Yeah, well let's hope they don't just slip under the ropes while all you guys are looking the other way, trying to outbid one another," Joe snapped.

"Not a chance, Riley. Nary a one."

"Couldn't a good defense attorney argue that with all those charges, they cancel one another out somehow?"

"How?"

"I don't know," Joe said, his voice ringing with irritation, "but that's what defense attorneys do, isn't it?"

"In la-la land, or on the tube, maybe. Believe me, Joe, these guys are off the streets permanently."

Joe suddenly felt ashamed of the way he'd snapped at Vatterott. The homicide detective had been more than just helpful, he'd been a friend. He didn't deserve to be a scapegoat for Joe's foul mood.

"Just riding you a little, Pete," Joe said, softening his tone with effort.

"How are the kids doing, Joe?"

Joe's breath caught in his throat. A wave of nausea assailed him. The question had come at him from out of left field, leaving him disoriented.

"I…uh…well, the truth is…uh, Pete…"

"You can speak plainer than that, Riley," he

mocked, and when Joe didn't answer, a hard edge crept into his voice. "What's going on, Joe?"

"The twins aren't mine," Joe blurted.

There was a pause and then Vatterott said, "Yeah, so?"

"You knew?"

The detective's laugh was mirthless. "Hey, I'm a cop. It's my job to know things."

"Well, then you know there wasn't anything for me to stick around for."

It was Vatterott's turn to grow silent. After a moment he said, "You're a real ass, Riley. I never would have guessed it."

Joe heard the click on the other end of the line and stared at the phone in his hand. Vatterott had hung up on him. He slammed the phone back in its cradle and threw himself down on the bed.

In the silence of the room he heard the digital clock on the radio shifting to the next number. He folded his arm over his eyes and tried to clear his mind of all thought.

"Hold my hand, Joe,"

"No, hold mine."

"I've got two hands, guys."

"You're my bestest friend in the whole world, Joe."

"Me, too. You're my bestest friend, too, Joe."

Joe groaned and turned over. He dragged a pillow down and covered his face with it.

They were going home tomorrow. That meant Ash was fully recovered, or at least out of danger. He wondered if Kate would rent a car or if they'd take the train. He remembered that he'd been carrying Robbie's little Santa bear when he and Vatterott had left the hotel in their mad rush to get to Yonkers. He wondered if it was still in the cop's car or if Vatterott had returned it to Robbie.

He shifted to his other side, moving the pillow as well.

"Joe, how come people get tan from the sun and not from the moon?"

"Joe, where do brown eggs come from?"

"I can eat five hangerburgers, Joe. Honest, I can."

"Robbie's telling a fib, Mommy. He can't eat five hangerburgers, can he?"

"I don't know, Ash, but I wouldn't want to be in the same room with him after he tried, would you?"

They'd all laughed at that, and Robbie had blushed when he got the joke.

Joe laughed now, remembering. And then he sobered and pounded his fist into the pillow.

"I can't wear any of my clothes, Mommy. They all make me nervous."

"Okay, Ash. But think how nervous everyone else is going to be when you show up in the hotel lobby naked as the day you were hatched out of that ostrich egg."

"You're so silly, Mommy. Maybe the blue overalls won't make me so-o nervous."

Didn't the woman ever raise her voice, ever get mad? Well, yeah, she could get pretty pissed at him.

And rightly so, Riley. Had he told her how special she was, how she brightened his days, excited his nights? Had he let her know how much he admired, respected, loved her.

Loved her?

He bolted up in the bed and looked around, a deranged expression on his face. He glimpsed it in the mirror on the credenza across from the bed. Why

shouldn't he look like a madman? Joe Riley in love?
Hah! He said it again, this time aloud.

"Hah!" What did he know about love? Nothing.
What he knew about love you could put in one of Ashleigh's dollhouse teacups.

He remembered pretending to drink out of one of
them. She'd offered him a choice of chocolate milk or
Scotch. She'd solemnly assured him it was okay because it was just make-believe. He'd asked for Scotch
and then pretended to get drunk and the twins had got
in the act, all three of them staggering around and slur-
ring their words and acting silly as hell until Kate had
threatened to send all three of them to their rooms for
time-out.

"Joe swore, Mommy. He did. He said the D-word."

*"Perhaps Joe doesn't mind being considered bad-
mannered and unintelligent."*

She'd said it calmly, without ever looking up from
the newspaper she was reading at the table. Joe had
been surprised at how shamed he'd felt, especially
when Ash had given him that pointed look of hers and
nodded her head wisely.

*"And then people won't enjoy your company any-
more, Joe."*

Kate had raised the paper in front of her face, but
he'd heard her giggle.

"God, I love her!" he said, clutching his hands to
his stomach. "I *D*-word well love her!"

He stood up and paced the small room. What if he
just went to Lake George, confronted her, told her he
loved her?

Would she believe him? Forgive him for his deceit?
He thought about the ways he'd deceived her. Following her like a second-rate private eye. Pretending he

was interested in chartering a boat. Pretending to be a journalist so he'd have an excuse to hang out at day care and be near the twins. And then even after he told her his real identity, he didn't tell her that he thought he might be the kids' father. Did she know he'd even suspected her of being involved in Monica's murder, maybe of stealing the twins?

But maybe even after all that, she'd forgive him when he told her how he felt about her.

He tried to imagine how she'd take his declaration of love. He drew a blank.

His loving her didn't mean she loved him back. He tried to recall if she'd said it while they were having sex. Women did that sometimes. Hell, a lot of men probably did, too. He knew he'd never done it, but then, he'd never really tried to impress any women with anything more promising than a steak dinner and a good bottle of wine.

He went to the window and peered out at the neon-lit night. New York—how he'd longed for it when he'd lain awake nights in his tent in the desert. And then he recalled how nothing had satisfied him when he'd looked at apartments with that Realtor. How he'd kept having those odd visions of houses and gardens.

A house like Kate's. Kids and Little League, picnics and Disney films, PTA meetings and friends like Mary-beth Simpson and her husband. He looked for the downside. And drew another blank.

It struck him then like a bolt of lightning. Those were the things Kate had to offer him. What did he have to offer her?

He stripped down to his shorts and got into bed. He'd better have an answer to that before he went, hat in hand, to Lake George.

Chapter Fifteen

Kate checked off the last item on the clipboard she carried and gave a thumbs-up to the captain who hung out of the pilot-house window at the top of the MV *Georgia*. He returned the signal from his lofty perch three stories up, and then tooted the foghorn a couple of times for emphasis.

Kate stepped off the gangplank and stood on the dock to watch the big paddlewheeler move away from the dock. The calliope was playing now and the charter guests were crowded at the rail, waving and laughing and generally getting revved for their party.

She turned, still smiling, and walked back to her office, confident that the crew and caterers would provide exactly the party the client had requested. Just the business of stopping to deposit the days' receipts at the bank, and then she could pick up the children and go home.

Valerie Masters was on the phone in her office. She lifted a hand to stop Kate on her way past. Kate waited as her assistant rang off and gestured her into the room, a silly grin on her face.

"Katie! Guess who that was?"

"What do I get if I guess right?" Kate slumped into

a chair beside Valerie's desk and propped her feet on the partially open file cabinet drawer.

The grin on Valerie's freckled face widened. "The question is, folks, what do *I* get if I sell a charter to Senator Grace for his family's annual reunion?"

Kate stared at her co-worker. "You did not!"

Valerie's grin was replaced by a solemn look. She raised her right hand, fingers forming the Girl Scout salute. "Swear."

"Get o-ver yourself, Masters! You didn't." Kate couldn't let herself believe what she was hearing. She leaned forward, gaping at Valerie.

Valerie stood up and bowed three times to an invisible audience. "Thank you, thank you. No autographs, please."

Kate jumped to her feet, laughing. "Senator Grace? Vallie, you've put us on the map, girlfriend!"

They high-fived, and then Kate gave Valerie an exuberant hug. "Ooh, Val, we've got to celebrate."

"I was thinking more along the lines of a raise," Val said.

"Both!"

Val sat down with a grin. "Yeah? Both? Really?"

Kate nodded, returning the grin and then some. "How about dinner at the Cove on Saturday night, for starters?"

"Good for me."

"Good." Kate stood up, picked up her clipboard and started out of the room. "You can pick up the check with your new raise," she called over her shoulder, and ducked just as a booklet came sailing at her from behind.

She was still laughing when she sat behind her own desk and reached for the ringing phone.

"Ms. Adams?" The voice sounded wary.

Kate sobered. There were few people who knew her real name, and all but one were connected with her recent ordeal.

"Speaking," she said warily.

"Pete Vatterott here. NYPD."

"Oh. Yes." She breathed a sigh of relief. "Detective Vatterott, what can I do for you?"

"The D.A. asked me to call and set up an appointment with you to make a statement. Your call—he can send someone up there or you come down to the city."

Kate took a deep breath. "You got the case, then."

"Yeah. After all the legal beagles sorted it out, it was agreed murder took priority, and since you were taken from a hotel here in the city, we were able to add the kidnapping charges to our indictment."

"They're going to be tried together?"

"Yeah." Vatterott chuckled. "They had one gun between the two of them. Sharing. And of course each one is accusing the other."

"I guess I could come down there." She turned the pages on her desk calendar, automatically judging which days she could free herself up for the whole day.

"How about Thursday?" she said. "I can be there around eleven."

"Thursday's good."

She was about to hang up when she heard the detective say something else. She asked him to repeat it.

"I wondered if you've heard anything from Joe Riley."

She felt the familiar lurch in her stomach and put her head down on the desk for a moment.

"Ms. Adams…Kate…are you there?"

She straightened up and took a steadying breath.

"Yes. I'm here. And no, I have not heard from Mr. Riley."

"Ah…I see."

"Has he…won't you need him to make a statement, too?"

"He's done that. I just wondered if…"

"No. He hasn't contacted us at all, and I really must go, Detective, my next appointment is here."

She hung up as he was repeating that he'd see her on Thursday.

Why would he expect Joe to contact her? She was sure that he knew by now that Joe had discovered he wasn't the twins' father. There'd be no reason to stay in touch. Whatever Joe had expected to gain by getting close to Kate, his reasons no longer existed.

After talking it over with Marybeth, she'd come to the conclusion that Joe's motive for making love to her had been to assure himself that she'd be willing to continue to play the role of mother to the children after he made his claim. It was one thing to claim paternity, another to take on a pair of six-year-olds and all the responsibilities and problems that entailed. A built-in mother would make the transition a whole lot easier for him.

Marybeth hadn't been convinced. "You think he'd stick himself with a woman he didn't love just to have a baby-sitter, a housekeeper, to help him with the kids? Sounds a little far-fetched to me. Besides, Joe Riley didn't strike me as the cold-blooded type, Kate."

"Cold-blooded enough to lie, to get the kids attached to him before he admitted why he was hanging around, to make love to a woman he doesn't love," Kate had argued.

Marybeth had only shaken her head, a sympathetic expression of sorrow on her face.

Kate shoved the phone away and reached for the bank deposit bag. She didn't want sympathy. Didn't need it. She still had her children and a job and friends she loved; a good life. That's all she needed.

The anger would pass, she told herself. But she didn't question where the anger came from or why she felt it. Whenever she started to think about it, the voice in her head warned, *"Don't go there!"*

She took the deposit pouch and her jacket and bag and left her office on the run, barely responding to Val's wave as she passed her open door.

JOE WATCHED KATE RUN across the street, holding her hand up to stop the car coming toward her. The driver slowed as Kate dashed to the curb and leaned out of his window to call out a warning to Kate. He saw her grin and heard her call back, "Thanks, Dr. Samuels, same for you sometime."

She walked briskly along the street, ignoring the shop windows she passed, her posture and speed suggesting a woman on a mission. Joe had spotted the bank pouch in her hand. He followed at a leisurely pace, knowing where she was headed.

He drew up alongside of the bank and peered into the front window. She was at a teller's cage, chatting with the young woman behind the window. Her red hair swung around her face as she gestured, and Joe had the weirdest sensation that he could actually smell her shampoo.

He hurried around the corner of the building when he saw that she had completed her business and was headed to the door.

He heard her heels clicking on the sidewalk as she moved down the street. He waited a minute and then slipped out to continue following her, knowing she was going in the direction of Kiddy Korner.

She was wearing a cotton suit with a short flared skirt, and he enjoyed the flash of leg as the skirt swung around her stride.

At the Rainbow Café she waved at the couple who were sitting in a window booth, and at the corner she stopped and talked to a little old Asian man who was sweeping the sidewalk in front of the video store. When she crossed over to Maple Avenue, the street on which the day-care center was located, she stopped to sniff the roses that hung in heavy clumps over the top of an iron picket fence surrounding the mayor's house.

Joe felt as if his heart were going to burst through his chest when a dog came running out at Kate from the yard next to the mayor's and jumped on her, barking furiously. But Kate laughed and let the dog leap up into her arms, laughing as the mid-size terrier licked her face and scrambled to stay in her arms. She put the dog down and scolded it for leaving the yard and then swung on her way down the street. The dog looked after her, his tail wagging sadly, but he stayed where he belonged.

Joe shook his head and put his hand to his chest, willing his heart to slow to its normal pace. He should have known she'd have the same calm, quiet control over dogs that she had over kids. He didn't think he'd ever seen her lose control or become overwrought by anything.

And then the image that had been haunting him for days flashed into his mind—the image of Kate, lying on that hotel bed and totally out of control as she called out his name and screamed her passion. Joe slumped against the mayor's fence, his legs weakening.

What if she turned around suddenly, saw him there? Would she run away? Stride toward him, telling him to leave her alone, threaten to call the cops? He stayed where he was and watched her go through the gate to Kiddy Korner. He couldn't confront her on the street. He had to bide his time, approach her on her own home ground where she had nowhere to run. He didn't expect her to forgive him, but by God he was going to have the chance to say what he had to say before she slammed the door in his face. And he couldn't corner her when she had the children around her; he would never do anything that might cause them unhappiness.

Joe turned, heading back to his motel. Suddenly he stopped. This was ridiculous, juvenile. How could it hurt the children to see Joe's real feelings? Maybe if he'd been more open from the beginning, he and Kate and the twins would be together as a family right now.

His gaze fell on the heavily-weighted rose bush, the branches bent almost to the sidewalk by their lush burden. Strictly speaking the roses that hung over the fence were on city property and as such belonged to the general public. Still, he looked around to make sure he was alone on the street as he took the Swiss army knife from his pocket and began cutting from the most outward branch.

KATE WAS WALKING backwards, still talking to Marybeth as the children skipped ahead.

Beth was propped on the porch rail. "You could at least call him while you're in the city on Thursday," Beth argued.

The discussion, bordering on debate, had been going

on for the last half hour and Marybeth was determined to get in the last word.

Out of the corner of her eye she noticed the twins bending to pick up something on the path, but she kept her attention on Marybeth, stopping her backward walk to stand still, her hands on her hips.

"And say what? What is there left to say? And how could I believe anything he said?"

"People make mistakes, Kate," Marybeth said softly. "I've never seen you like this, so stubbornly judgmental."

"Judgmental? How can you say…"

"Mommy, look at all the beautiful flowers," Robbie said, pulling on Kate's shirt.

"Just a minute, honey," Kate said, without turning. "I'm talking to Marybeth."

But Marybeth had slipped down off the rail, pushed her eyeglasses down from the top of her head and was peering at something behind Kate.

"I really resent you using that word, girlfriend, after all…"

Her words trailed away on a note of puzzlement as Marybeth strode toward and then past her. The children were chattering about flowers and when Marybeth reached them, her voice joined with theirs.

Kate turned. The length of the sidewalk, from the bottom step of the porch to the gate, was strewn with rose petals. Her first thought was that while she was absorbed by her argument with Marybeth, the twins had pulled the roses from the mayor's bush and littered the path with torn petals.

"Oh, no," she wailed. "You didn't take the mayor's roses!"

Ashleigh looked up, her hands full of petals, her face

set in an expression of outrage. "We didn't do this, Mommy. They were here when we came out."

Kate turned to Marybeth. "Who in the world would have done this?" she asked, puzzled.

Marybeth looked down at the sidewalk and then back at Kate. A smile broke on her face and began to laugh.

"I don't know," she whispered between giggles. "Maybe I have a secret admirer."

Kate frowned. "But everybody in town knows you're married."

Marybeth was too busy laughing to respond to that.

"Come on, kids," Kate said, nudging the children ahead of her. "Aunt Marybeth is having one of her crazy spells."

The gate opened onto a continuing array of the flower petals. The children were stooping to gather them up, shoving them into their overall pockets.

"Cut that out," Kate said, feeling strangely irritated. "If you don't get all of those petals out of those pockets they're going to clog up the washing machine."

"We'll get 'em all out," Robbie said. "We're gonna use 'em to build a beautiful bird's nest."

"Only a bird can build a bird's nest," Kate said absently, her focus on the streak of red that led like an arrow right up the street and seemed endless to her view.

The children grew more and more excited over the rose carpet beneath their feet and made a game of kicking the petals aside as they would with fallen leaves. Kate was barely aware of their chatter. The fragrance of the flowers rose up to tease her nostrils and her heart was beginning to thump erratically as she fought to suppress the realization that the path of flowers was leading directly to her own house.

As they approached the Chalmers house, Mrs. Chalmers' car was backing into the street. Kate and the twins were forced to halt at the edge of her driveway. The woman was a third grade teacher at the children's school, and she stopped the car and called to the trio.

"Has it been raining roses?" she solemnly asked the twins. They looked up at the sky, their mouths agape, and then realized the teacher was joking.

"Hi, Kate, how are you doing?" the woman asked, still chuckling over the momentary look of awe on the children's faces.

"Doin' fine, Samantha, how about you?"

"One more week until school starts and it still feels like summer, which means the little darlings are going to be distracted and won't settle in until the first real cold assures them summer, and their vacation, is over."

Kate grinned, glad for a moment to think about something but the dread that filled her as they drew closer to home.

"I know, the leaves haven't even begun to turn yet. Looks like we're going to have an unusually long season in the cruise business as well."

"Well, that's good for you, isn't it?"

"Yes. Sure. I don't look forward to the long, lonely winters when all I have to do is catch up on bookwork and take reservations for next spring."

"But look at the up side—you have more time than any of the other parents to volunteer for field trips and committees, and stuff."

Kate made a face at her friend. "Oh, yeah, how could I forget the up side," she jeered.

Samantha Chalmers laughed, waved and drove off after making sure the twins were out of the way.

Kate looked up the street; the peak of her roof was now in view and as far as she could tell the petal carpet led at least that far.

She couldn't even drag her feet and make the walk last, with the children pulling at her hands and urging her to "Come on, Slow Poke."

Kate's sense of dread mixed with a feeling of excitement, and created havoc in her stomach when they arrived at their own gate and saw that the flowers stopped short in front and then made a curve up the path to the front door.

Robbie was already racing up the stone path, Ashleigh hard on his heels as Kate took time to shut the gate. She called out to them to take it easy before somebody fell and got hurt, but they were already tearing through the front door betting each other about where the flowers would end.

"They're never going to end," Robbie panted. "They're going straight up the chimney and up to the sky!"

"Are not," Ashleigh bellowed. "They're going down to the basement and right down through the ground to China!"

Kate's involuntary laughter ceased when she heard the sound of footsteps coming around the side of the house. Her heart seemed to rise to her throat and her ears fill with a painful roar.

Joe stepped into view and suddenly everything inside of her seemed to reverse; she felt numb, unable to move as if her feet were cemented to the path.

The twins brought her out of her trance as they ran

out of the house screaming Joe's name and flinging themselves at him.

Kate watched as Joe knelt to embrace them, almost falling over as they assailed him with hugs, kisses and endless squeals of delight. She could remember quite clearly how she'd felt in the past when she observed the three of them together, yet now she couldn't raise a single feeling at the sight.

Joe's eyes met hers over the children's heads and he paled at the sight of her expression.

Gently he unwound the children's arms from his neck and got to his feet. In a quiet voice he said, "Would you guys go into the house and watch TV while I have a little talk with your mother?"

The children started to protest.

"You won't leave us again, will you, Joe?" Robbie asked.

"Please don't go way while we're in the house, Joe," Ashleigh pleaded.

"I promise I won't ever go away without telling you first." It was the best he could do for the moment. His sense of Kate's mood was that this wasn't going to be as easy as he'd hoped.

The children held each other's hands and shuffled toward the house, their heads bowed.

Rose petals scattered out of the way of their sneakers, but the twins were no longer excited by them.

Joe felt his eyes tearing up and he had to blow his nose and clear his throat before he turned back to Kate.

"Aren't you going to say anything, Kate?"

"What are you doing here?"

Joe's heart plummeted. Her tone was as expressionless as her face. Even if he could be his most articulate, most romantic, would it penetrate the wall of ice that seemed to encapsulate her?

He straightened to his full height and took a deep breath. He had to try.

"I wanted a chance to talk to you, to explain…"

Kate felt herself come to life with the force of her anger. In the past weeks since returning home, she hadn't been able to think of Joe Riley without experiencing intense pain. For the umpteenth time she silently repeated the mantra that had kept the pain at bay: *I deserve better!*

"How are you going to explain running away without a word, giving no thought to m…to the twins' feelings? How are you going to explain using me to get to them?"

"Kate, if you'll just give me a chance…"

"Give you a chance!" Kate almost screamed the words. And then she spotted the twins kneeling in the window of the living room, gloomily staring out at Kate and Joe.

She lowered her voice but used a sarcastic tone to emphasize the words.

"Hel-lo? Aren't you the same guy I ran off with in the middle of the night, no questions asked? The same guy I trusted with my kids? Didn't I steal a key and illegally enter an apartment with you? And let me see, do I vaguely recall hopping into bed with you for a little afternoon recreation?"

Joe cringed, but he kept his gaze locked on hers, refusing to back down. Her green eyes were shooting glints of gold, and if they'd been arrows, they'd have hit and blinded him.

"Add 'em up, Riley. More chances than a lying, low-bellied snake like you deserves."

Perspiration dampened his skin and his mind almost shut down. Helplessly he watched Kate turn to leave.

"I love you, Kate," he said softly, almost to himself.

Kate's foot touched down and then lifted as she pivoted to face him, a frown on her face.

"What did you say?"

"I said, I love you."

They stared into each other's faces, Kate searching his for sincerity, Joe searching hers for trust. She looked wary. He looked uncomfortable.

How could he expect her to drop all her charges against him in the bat of an eye, just because he'd said he loved her?

But with all his lies, he'd told her plenty of truths, she remembered. He had truly hurt when he learned of Matt Wilkins's death. And who could doubt his love for the twins—even after he learned they weren't his.

She closed her eyes for a moment as the image of his face looking down into hers, as they made love, almost blinded her in its intensity.

Kate took a step forward.

Joe stayed where he was, holding his breath.

Kate realized he had nothing to gain by lying now. She studied his grave face, read the vulnerability there. *And everything to lose.*

She took another step, her hand lifting at her side.

Inside the house, huddled up to the window overlooking the front yard, the twins held their breath and kept their fingers crossed.

"Are they going to make up, Ash?" Robbie asked.

"I dunno. Whenever we asked about Joe Mommy got real quiet, remember?"

Robbie nodded. "Does she hate Joe, do ya think?"

Ashleigh turned and punched her brother on the arm. "Nobody could ever hate Joe, you dummy."

Robbie sniffled and rubbed his arm. But he wasn't going to cry. Suddenly he knew Ashleigh couldn't make him cry anymore. He was a big boy. Mommy and Joe both said so. He punched his sister back, enjoying the look of surprise on her face.

"That didn't even hurt," Ashleigh said, turning back to the window. But it had and though she wasn't going to rub it in front of Robbie, she sure was going to make sure he didn't get another chance to...

Ashleigh gasped. "Robbie! Look! Look!"

Kate had closed the distance between her and Joe and his arms opened to enfold her. She leaned into his warmth, his strength, his love, and let all the reserves of bitterness and distrust fade away.

"Home at last," Joe whispered against the silken curls of her hair.

Kate nodded and lifted her head for his kiss. It was everything she remembered. And more. There was tenderness, desire, and in only moments...passion. The "more" was love, and Kate's heart opened to accept it with eagerness.

When the kiss ended they stared into each other's eyes, letting their silent message seal their bond. It was then Kate thought of Springer, a thought that had been bothering her for weeks.

"Joe, we're going to have to tell Springer, aren't we?"

Joe frowned and caressed Kate's cheek. "I don't think it will make a difference to him, really. Do you?"

"No, I don't think he'll want to claim the children."

Joe shook his head. "It doesn't matter. I'm prepared

to fight with everything I've got in me to protect you and the children. And speaking of the rugrats…''

He gestured toward the window where the twins were giving each other a high five. Kate knew then that the future held hope and the promise of happily ever after.

WHAT'S SEXIER THAN A COWBOY?
Three cowboy *brothers!*

HARLEQUIN®

INTRIGUE®
presents

A new trilogy by
bestselling author

PATRICIA ROSEMOOR

On a mission to save the family ranch and
make peace with each other, the Quarrels
boys are back in Silver Springs—but a
hidden danger threatens all they hold
dear, including their very lives!

Coming Spring 2000:

March: #559 HEART OF A LAWMAN
April: #563 THE LONE WOLF'S CHILD
May: #567 A RANCHER'S VOW

Available at your favorite retail outlet.

HARLEQUIN®
Makes any time special ™

Romance is just one click away!

love scopes

➤ Find out all about your guy in the Men of the Zodiac area.

➤ Get your daily horoscope.

➤ Take a look at our Passionscopes, Lovescopes, Birthday Scopes and more!

join Heart-to-Heart, our interactive community

➤ Talk with Harlequin authors!

➤ Meet other readers and chat with other members.

➤ Join the discussion forums and post messages on our message boards.

romantic ideas

➤ Get scrumptious meal ideas in the Romantic Recipes area!

➤ Check out the Daily Love Dose to get romantic ideas and suggestions.

Visit us online at

www.eHarlequin.com

on Women.com Networks

HEUT2